Satyr

A Cozy Romantic Fantasy
Megan G. Mossgrove

Megan G. Mossgrove

SATYR

A COZY ROMANTIC FANTASY

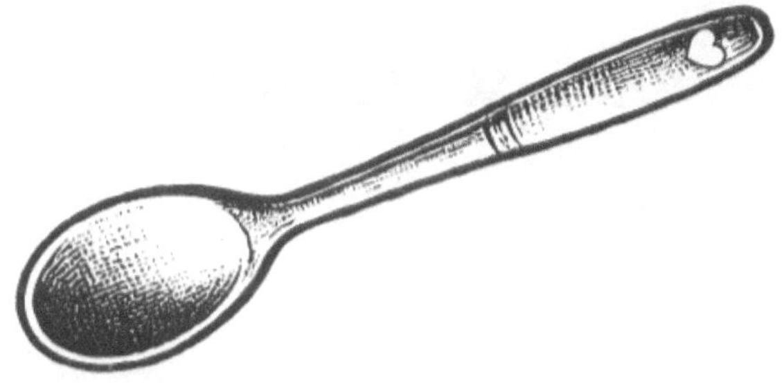

MEGAN G. MOSSGROVE

More By the Author

Atlas World Novels

Satyr, a Cozy Fantasy Romance

The Sundered Stone Trilogy

The Wingbreaker
The Prince of Pearls, coming 2025!

Author's Note

This book is a great fit for fans of cozy romantasy. The stakes are fairly low, **though there is some content I'd like to be very clear about for the sake of my readers**---Elaine, our FMC, cannot have children. She is in a time of transition after years of attempts and losses that ended in separating from her partner. While there is no loss on page, her identity is shaped with this in mind, and it does impact the story and her inner dialogue. There is also an on-page childbirth, it is complicated, but not graphic (and it is NOT Elaine).

Otherwise, there is off-page parent death, grief, and a small bit of strong language.

*This book is **low spice**, but not no spice!*

For those who have carried a baby
they never held in their arms.

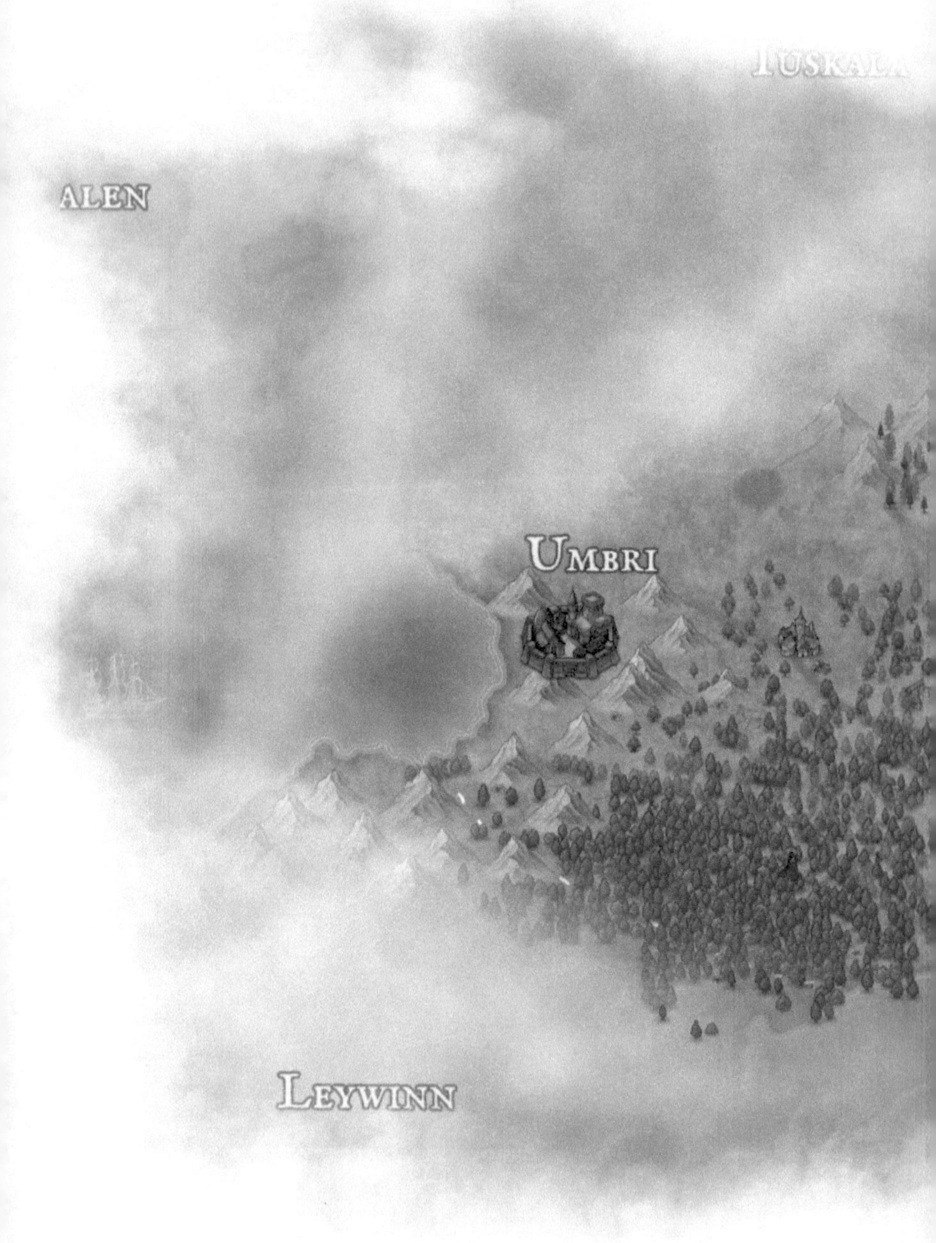

TUSKALA
ALEN
UMBRI
LEYWINN

Moordia
Arnell
Corsair
Mire Isles
THE ATLAS WORLD

1

Elaine

ELAINE HARDLY HUMMED ANYMORE, but this was a good day for it.

The kitchen staff bustled around placing garnishes as the servers flitted through the swinging door, snatching dishes to present to the royal family and the delegation from Corsair.

"Wait, wait, wait!" She scurried to the tray and pulled a few nasturtiums to tuck next to the glazed duck. "Thank you, Neena." The serving girl smiled, forever patient, as Elaine ensured the main course was just right.

The door swung open and closed again, favoring her with a puff of cooler air. The dish was perfect, she could *feel* it. She turned a satisfied grin on her staff, but they were busy cleaning—eager to get home.

Over the past month, they'd all seemed to quietly agree to finish the day and leave quickly. Tensions had been high since the princess's disappearance. Interrogations . . . outbursts from the king. She didn't want to stay any longer than they did. She grabbed a towel and joined the staff, stacking dishes and wiping counters.

"Do you need any help here?" Elaine asked, placing the clinking tower of pans next to Roman, their newest wash boy.

"No, miss, thank you."

She nodded, then turned to address the room. "I'm going down to the traveler's market this evening. Would anyone care to join?"

"Maybe next time," Airam said as he adjusted a hood over a waterfall of inky braids and pointed ears. "I told the husband we could make plans."

The others echoed similar sentiments, and Elaine had to rush to get her things before following them out the door. Chill, salty air kissed her skin. The castle gardens always looked exceptionally beautiful in the soft evening light; spring flowers showed off their proud colors, nasturtiums and snapdragons blooming just as the daffodils died back. She was tempted, but didn't dally, instead choosing to catch up with her friends—well, *friends* was a strong word. The fae cooks had been working together since long before she'd arrived. Her initial employment began just days after her twenty-second birthday and, in the twelve years since, they'd been . . . cordial. But were also close knit and a hundred years her senior, though you could never tell by looking at them. Airam, at least, had warmed to her. She hadn't given up on the others.

Dubious of walking alone, she hovered at the edge of the group as they led the way down the main road from the castle. Her eyes fell as they walked, watching her patched shoes peek out from under her worn dress with every step. She should really get new ones; could have afforded it, but it seemed vain or disingenuous. The tattered nature of what she had fit better, somehow. How dramatic to doubt one is deserving of a new pair of shoes.

Plus, it would be hard to let go of the old ones.

Elaine waved her goodbye as they turned toward the residential district, while she carried on. The sun would set soon, and the crowded roads thinned out as the deeper cold crept in with the night. Near the market, she slowed, trying to hide the heaviness of her breathing. All her life she'd hated walking alone, especially in the dark, but the nature of her employment at the castle meant it was the only time she was free during the shorter days of the year. And it was better than going home.

She leapt forward as someone stepped on the back of her heel.

"Oh, excuse me."

Elaine turned to give the stranger a quick, obligatory smile and tried to subtly fix her shoe by tapping her toe on the ground. "That's quite alright. I shouldn't be in the way."

"Oh, it was completely my fault, my lady—" The girl trailed off as she took note of the dirty apron and worn gray dress. "Apologies, miss . . . I like your ribbon!" The girl offered a dazzling smile, but the older woman behind her, finely dressed in a white ruffled shirt and brocade skirts, gave her a nervous look and steered the young woman away by the shoulders.

Elaine, suddenly self-conscious, pulled her hair over one shoulder, mindlessly stroking the priceless silk the princess had gifted her the month before. She'd taken to banding it over her head and through her braid. It was conspicuous and completely impractical, but it was hers. As she walked, a few more gave her long, sideways looks, noticing the odd combination of the Dagadan silk and her working attire, but she ducked her head and carried on, aiming for her favorite spice cart.

"Elaine!" The Umbri trader grinned and gestured to a cart a few stops down. "Did you see we brought more oil blends? We've got extra rosemary and lemon just for you."

"The princess herself requested them!" Elaine exclaimed. "I've already added more to the order. Restock is tomorrow. I'll make sure the list goes out then."

The man sobered immediately. "The princess . . . I can't believe she still hasn't returned. It's a tragedy."

Elaine pressed her lips together as she nodded, unwilling to acknowledge the curiosity in the man's eyes. Instead, she turned her attention to the tiny labels on the spice bottles. She wouldn't be discussing the princess's disappearance. Not least of all because Elaine had aided her escape.

2

Satyr

THE ASPEN INN WAS all warm wood and delicious smells. Tucked on a side road away from the bustle of the market square, it attracted those who preferred simple, solid comfort over the more luxurious—and crowded—inns. Satyr had taken over the building after he 'retired,' and made a point to decorate it in the Tuskalan style, to bring the beauty of his home to Arnell to share with others. Many marveled over the orb-shaped paper lanterns that hung in clusters from the ceiling, or the mammoth-fur rugs in the rooms. The windows were larger than you'd find in Tuskala, but he'd commissioned decorative latticework typical of his homeland all the same. Satyr favored clay dishware and stone cookware over delicate glass or polished metals, and many, of course, appreciated the orc-sized wooden steins. He placed two in front of the waiting silk fae, her pale, blue-tinted skin and bright, appreciative smile contrasting her wide black eyes.

"Fáilte!" he called in greeting as a half-dwarf patron shuffled in from the cold, their thick hands tattooed down to the tips of their fingers, the design continuing past their wrist and disappearing under their long tunic sleeves.

There were a handful of dinner guests, and two of their rooms had occupants—pretty good for the middle of the week. He grinned, and the thick tusks on either side of his mouth pressed into his cheeks. The inn broke even only half the time, but that didn't stop him from loving the travelers who came, or the music the fae bard, Thorin, strummed on his lyre. The song was familiar now, and he hummed along softly as the man sang.

The water, she sees me
The waves bid me come
Come and then be free
Her beckoning hum
Were I to go, I'd ne'er return
The water, its song bid me stay
Stay and don't suffer for absence of land
Nought, but heartache lay that way

Sibyl tried skirting past him. "Excuse me, sir."

"Here, wait." He took the tray she held. It was heavy, stacked high with dirty cups and plates. "Would you mind checking on the corner booth?"

The corner booth was fine, and they both knew it. "Alright, but we're out of dill, too."

"On it," Satyr said as she waddled away. Her round belly made her dress flag out awkwardly as she turned. She was too far along to carry a tray bought with an orc's strength in mind.

Satyr pulled his thoughts from the immediate worries a child would bring, to her life especially. She'd been working at the inn as a trade for room and board, but he'd wondered more often than he should what she planned to do once the babe arrived.

He set the tray in the kitchen before heading out the back door. The brisk air swept right through his tunic and apron, washing away the heat from the ovens. He pulled the night deep into his lungs, savoring the hint of salty ocean. He could nearly taste the sea.

The owner of the next shop over was sweeping a mess out her back door. He gave the faun an obligatory nod and a polite smile. Jewels glittered as she moved, strung on chains that wove between her antlers. He always wondered if they were real. Hers was the curiosities shop on this street, but if anyone ever visited, he'd never noticed. She didn't smile back, instead pushing her head up and over as if she'd spotted something behind him. One of her long, fuzzy ears flicked in nervous tandem with her tail.

Satyr scanned the street but saw nothing.

"Have a wonderful day, Ayala," he called over his shoulder as he carried on, feeling foolish for the spark of nerves the woman always gave him. She often offered to read his tea leaves, but he'd decided long ago to live unchained from an ambiguous, unpromised future. Did he believe in fortune telling? Maybe more than he'd admit.

All the more reason not to do it.

The market still bustled despite the setting sun, and traders would continue to peddle their wares until long after it set. He aimed for his favorite spice cart, stepping delicately, returning any nervous glances with his most charming smile. He was at least a head taller than most of the crowd that split to let him pass, many doing their best to hide curious or nervous looks. Carefully, he turned his body and edged in near the spice merchant, so as not to touch the noblewoman already looking over the spices. "Gregor!" he called, loud enough to be heard over the constant hum of voices.

The Umbri trader snapped his head up from the woman's perusing. "Satyr! Good to see you again—what'll it be this fine evening?"

"It seems I've run out of dill. Got any?" The merchant only attended the traveler's market a week out of every month, despite Satyr's attempts to convince him to rent a permanent slot.

The man nodded and flicked his fingers over the tinkling glass jars. "Just one?"

"Make it three. And also—" Satyr twisted each to see the labels, trying to recall if he needed anything else.

His heart leapt as he spotted it, tucked in the middle, powdery red. He reached for the jar just as the noblewoman did, and their fingers tangled over it. He looked down at her in surprise.

Warm brown eyes flashed in defiance then widened slightly as she took him in. A slow flush crawled up her neck, into her cheeks, reddening her moonlight skin. All he could do was smile, trying not to scare her further.

"Gregor." Satyr didn't look at the fae man. Neither did the woman. Her hands were cool and soft under his fingers. "Is there a second jar of paprika?"

"I'm afraid that's the only one." He could hear the wince in the trader's voice.

"We'll split it." The woman's voice was light. Flowery. But the words were less an offer and more of a command. Satyr's smile was genuine now, a small heat pooling in his stomach as she refused to pull her hand or eyes away from his.

"We'll split it," he affirmed. Gregor knelt, jangling supplies around as he looked for an empty jar. The woman's chest rose and fell with a steadying breath and she smiled politely. He'd been wrong—she wasn't a noble. She wore an apron as stained as his own, and her blonde hair, while shining with the luxurious Dagadan silk, was more disheveled than he'd noticed before. Small cuts and burns betrayed her further—he recognized the evidence of a passionate chef, as the marks were mirrored on his own green hands. Her smile curled from politeness into something genuine. Recognizing a kindred spirit?

Gregor cleared his throat, reaching for the spice bottle, and Satyr hesitated a beat before lifting his hand away. As the merchant carefully tapped an even amount into each, he threw a look at the oil cart. "I'm not sure you should wait on the oils, Elaine. They're in high demand this year."

The woman, Elaine, gave him a coin for the paprika and flashed Satyr a dazzling grin. "I hope it's delicious," she said, waving her bottle in farewell before going that way, her long braid swishing across her back.

"The lemon oils?" Satyr asked the merchant as he watched her go.

"Yes, she always orders a lot for the castle when we're here, but it looks like we may run out even with the extras."

Satyr plunked a few coins onto the counter and followed in her footsteps, already brainstorming what to say. The lemon oil really was excellent, especially with fish. Surely that was a good place to start? But she was already in conversation when he caught up with her.

"How many did you need, miss?"

"As many as I can carry."

"As many as the two of us can carry, if you'd like," Satyr interrupted, surprising himself with his boldness.

Her lips parted as he stepped beside her, a curious line between her brows. He shrugged, suddenly shyer than he'd been since he was a child. "Gregor mentioned you work for the castle, so you'll need plenty. Please consider my help a thank you for splitting the paprika. My inn has been out since the winter began."

"Oh, I couldn't possibly trouble you. And really, there's no need to thank me. In fact—thank you!" Her face was positively crimson, her brown eyes wide. Glass jostled as the merchant placed the goods on the counter.

His chest hollowed out, but only slightly. He couldn't blame her for her nerves. He was, undoubtedly, imposing. "I see. I wouldn't dream of pressing a lady further. I apologize for my boldness, have a lovely day." He nodded farewell and turned back toward the crowds. Oils for the inn could wait until tomorrow.

A cool hand grasped his forearm, but she ripped it away as soon as he looked back. The sack's awkward bulk looked even heavier as she eased it down, her knuckles already white against the weight. "You're certain it would be no trouble?"

Truthfully, he should return to the inn. He certainly shouldn't go to the castle, which would take him well out of his way. Yet, he found himself reaching down, easing the sack from her grip. She held on for a moment, her eyes flickering over him as he spoke.

"I'm certain it would be worthy trouble."

There was a sprinkling of light freckles over her nose, standing out against skin as fair as the moon. The pearly pink silk brought out the color in her cheeks. Her lips were plump and deliciously curvy—like the rest of her. Rounded ears peeked out from under her tousled braid. Human.

"The name's Satyr," he said, suddenly unable to think of anything more impressive.

"I'm Elaine." Her lips curled up even as her gaze flitted to the ground, away from his blatant assessment. She released the bag, hands clasping in front of her.

Too bold again.

But her smile was bright as she ordered more.

3

Elaine

"So, you work in the castle kitchens?"

Elaine nodded, petrified and remarkably mute as they walked through the crowded market. Her voice had stopped working the moment she realized she was leading a male back to her home while the sun was truly on its way to setting.

"And the king likes paprika?"

That jolted a laugh out of her. "Well, he's never complained."

The orc offered a tense smile. He had a square-ish face, and a strong jaw lined with meticulously trimmed facial hair—black, like the loose bun tied at the back of his head. The color contrasted the soft green of his skin. The shaved sides of his hair revealed pointed ears that must be as long as her middle finger. And he had tusks of course.

How did he kiss with those?

13

Elaine blinked, trying to reign in that wayward thought. Still, she couldn't help noticing the way his thick neck sloped into strong shoulders, and the sleeveless brown tunic he wore freely displayed the sculpted nature of his arms, one of which flexed due to its burden of oils.

She blushed, but he didn't notice her assessment. He kept his head up and had stiffened as they walked, spine rigid now. His voice remained overly gentle when greeting those who stared or gave them a second look.

Or a third.

Some smiled back, others gave them a wide berth. No matter their reaction, he kept that same strained smile on his face and met the next eye to nod a greeting.

"Do you always do that?" She wanted to suck the words back in. Instead, she pinned her gaze ahead, hoping he couldn't see her blazing cheeks in the fading light.

"Do what?"

"Pretend like you aren't bothered by others being odd?" Elaine was well above average height for a woman, just a couple inches shorter than six feet, but he was still a head taller, and strangers' eyes seemed to track their movement through the crowd. His confusion eased into understanding and his shoulders curled forward, the gesture at odds with his powerful body. He raked a hand through his hair, disturbing the bun.

"My hope is to set them at ease. It's not every day you find an orc wearing an apron and wandering the market. I understand

I may be . . ." He shrugged and lifted a palm as an offering. The bagged bottles jingled over his shoulder. "Scary? A sight to behold?"

His cheeks darkened as she snorted. "The first, no," she said. "The second? Most definitely." She beamed, but the surprise on his face clamped her lips together and she refused to acknowledge his probing looks as she forged ahead. "So, your patrons like paprika?"

"*I* like paprika. I have an old family recipe for duck I've been craving, but with the drought and early winter . . ." he trailed off. "Were we not going to the castle?"

Elaine swallowed. They'd turned into the residential district. Had she said they'd take the bottles to the castle? "No, I was hoping to take them to my home. The walk is shorter, and my mornings start early." She stopped, and suddenly he was facing her again, but she wasn't going to assume—"Is that okay?"

"Are you sure that's okay with you? I can hold these at The Aspen Inn."

"You mean if I'm worried about the scary male knowing where I live?" she crooned, but immediately slapped a hand over her mouth, aghast by her playful tone. He laughed, but she shook her head. "I'm sorry. I'm not usually like this." Not for a while anyway.

Elaine hefted the weight of the second bag of oils between each of her hands. He took it without a word and held it easily, along with the others. "I really do appreciate your help. It would be a tragedy to miss out for the whole month. Plus, I hate walking alone." She clasped her hands and bowed slightly. "And I'm sorry for teasing you."

"Don't apologize, Elaine. In Tuskala, verbal sparring is vital to our friendships, so it's a comfort. Will your"—he cleared his throat, his voice taking on a peculiar edge"—ah, family be concerned to see me?"

The unexpected question sent a pang through her chest.

4

Satyr

"I don't have a family."

Satyr felt he'd mis-stepped. She'd gone stiff, her steps suddenly clipped.

"I don't either. Not here." She pierced him with a suspicious look, and he fumbled over his need to clarify. "No wife at all I mean, and no children." No male worth his salt would abandon a family to live in a different kingdom. "Family is the most important thing to an orc. We are a loyal, protective people, and proud of our own."

She nodded. "Well, no matter—here we are," she sighed, avoiding his eyes and squaring herself against a thin two-story home squeezed between others of similar size. The cheery-yellow wood was complemented by small windows trimmed with clean white, but the flower boxes underneath the panes were conspicuously empty—as were the large, soil-filled pots on either side of the door.

She efficiently fitted a key in the lock, stoic as a weathered soldier, and winced when the door whined on its hinges. Once through the threshold, she didn't speak or look back. To the immediate left, a staircase led to the second floor, and a little ways down on the right, a door stood open, allowing him a glimpse of a minimalistic sitting room.

Satyr stood awkwardly in the hallway, unsure if he should follow, or if her sudden change in demeanor meant she regretted bringing him to her home after all. He'd just decided to leave the bottles and go when she reappeared, hands busy untying the stained apron around her waist.

"Just back here, if you don't mind."

Her smile was back, muted by the unnamed shadow that'd befallen her as they'd arrived, and, as uncertain as the change made him, it also drew him forward, curious and melancholy. No. It wasn't her that made him feel that way.

It was the house.

As he passed, he realized the sitting room wasn't minimalistic—it was bare. A heavy blanket and pillow were scrunched on the sofa, the low table littered with empty mugs. Areas of heavy dust and those with marginally less indicated where previous furniture rested but appeared long since removed. The hallway was free of portraits or decoration, and the naked floor meant every movement was overly loud, the creaks echoing against the emptiness of the home.

He followed her through the far door, stepping lightly, loath to elicit the board's protestations, absurdly concerned his weight might be enough to send him through the floor.

"Just on the counter, there, please," she said, tucking the half-full paprika into a crowded spice rack. But he'd stopped short, surprised. The kitchen burst with color and living things. Plants graced every flat surface, the windowsill, the counter, the breakfast table tucked to one side. Strips of cloth hung in a rainbow of colors on one wall, and another artfully displayed kitchen utensils hanging on heavy duty hooks.

He placed the bags on the counter and began to unload the oils, their elbows brushing as she slid beside him and grabbed one. The causal touch sent an electric shock through him.

"What?" she asked, her smile genuine now. He schooled his features, pushing down the surprise.

"You have a beautiful kitchen."

She smiled, pouring the lemon oil into a stone skillet resting on a now-lit grate. "You don't mind if I feed you for your help, do you? I'm starving." She turned and her voice was muffled as she wrestled something out of the ice box. "And it's the best way I know how to thank someone. My sister says it's a love language."

Try as he might, Satyr was slow to rein in his gaping. He'd absolutely been gone from the inn too long as it was.

And he'd rather wrestle a manticore than decline that offer.

He managed to close his mouth just as she halted, brows pinching in sudden doubt with his silence.

"By all means," he said. "How can I help?"

"No help needed at all, you're welcome to have a seat." She tucked stray wisps of hair behind her soft ears and washed her hands before sourcing a variety of root vegetables from a wrapped woven basket on the counter.

He eyed the single, small chair at the breakfast table, and decided he'd be better off standing. In fact—He washed his own hands and picked up the knife she'd placed by the vegetables. "Sliced or quartered?" he asked as she moved to pluck springs from the various herbs under the window.

She glanced his way and her lips turn up on one side. "Quartered, please." Now, fish sizzled in the hot oil and she began mincing the herbs. "Would you mind a bold question?" The Dagadan silk in her hair shimmered in the flickering candlelight as the very last of the sunlight finally fled.

Something in his gut tightened with anticipation, but his hands never faltered. The turnips were done, now the rutabaga.

"If you're feeding me, you can ask anything you want."

She laughed. "You're helping."

"A question for a question then?" he asked, not at all certain where his loose lips planned to go with that.

"Deal. So, what makes an orc open an inn? Don't you usually, that is to say, don't . . . orcs prefer, ah. Um. More adventurous work?" The pitch of the words went up steadily as she spoke, and she cringed at the herbs enough that he couldn't help the bellowing laugh that erupted from deep in his belly. She jumped like a frightened cat and he reached out to reassure her as he doubled over with the force of his mirth, the sound as magnified as the creaks of the floor.

"You could barely get the words out," he boomed, before sobering, realizing he'd rested a too-large hand on her delicate forearm. "Sorry." He let go, returning his attention to the vegetables, but the laugh bubbled up again. "I thought you were going to jump out of your skin. I'm loud on a quiet day, and your home makes everything louder."

"It does," she agreed, but he didn't trust the bright tone.

"Sorry." He was used to speaking over lyres and clanking dishes.

"Don't be. It's nice."

He paused to look at her, but she'd already turned to the fish again, flipping it to sprinkle herbs on both sides.

After a moment, he chanced speaking again, keeping his volume low. "I moved to Arnell after serving Tuskala for over a decade. I was good at it. Skirmishes mostly, sometimes on the northern border, but often independent clans or pirates from the grass sea would test their luck against our steel. It's true, orcs do enjoy a little internal conflict and in the past our culture demanded it. Each of us serves at least three years. About four years ago, my youngest brother wanted out before his contract was up. And I helped him disappear. After that it . . . became necessary for me to leave." Satyr had told the tale a hundred times before.

Now, he wondered if his matter-of-fact tone made him seem heartless or unmoved by the experience. That wasn't the case of course. When Jondur defected, he'd joined a band of pirates, shaming their family twice in one act. The betrayal rocked their lives, and Satyr was forced to flee as his brother's accomplice. The inn was a fluke. He'd gotten lucky. Had spent a year brawling for coin in certain illicit betting rings until finding steady employment in Arnell's shipping district. He wasn't the only orc in Arnell, but he might be the only one that wasn't offering his sword for hire in an effort to gain abstract glory.

That part of his life was over.

"In the end," he continued, pushing the finished vegetables her way. "I relied on the charity of an old fae couple. The husband was a fisherman, and he was getting to the point of needing help. I helped." Fisherman was the more polite word. The old man was a pearl skimmer—a licensed boatman permitted to harvest the reef's magical components in the name of the crown—except, in his case, it turned to smuggling. When he retired, he convinced a few others to do the same in his absence—for a percentage of the profit.

"And they ran the inn too?" she pressed. The fish sizzled now, and she'd scooped the veggies away from him as well.

"No. That was all me." When he'd agreed to buy it, he was starry-eyed and determined to grow it into something successful enough to stand on its own. "I'm still making payments." He sighed, moving to scrub at the dishes in the sink. The inn hadn't quite made it there, yet. But the smuggling kept them afloat while he continued to try, though it was a distraction as much as it was a boon. "Probably will be for the rest of my life," he admitted. "But as long as the travelers bring their stories, the bards bring their music, and I have reason to cook, what more could I ask for?"

She huffed a laugh as she plated their dinner. "No argument there. But if I'd have known I would need to impress another cook, I'd have taken an extra day to prepare. I don't keep much at home, it's not worth it to go through the effort just for me."

"That's a shame; it smells divine."

She gestured for him to follow and he tried not to look around too curiously as they went back down the hall. She sat the plates down in the sitting room and gathered the used mugs from the table before the sofa and left, leaving him to study the perfectly seared fish and remarkably empty room. By the time she returned, he knelt before the fireplace.

"Oh. I should have thought of that." She settled on the sofa, curling herself into the thick blanket. Even the half-full stack of wood seemed dusty.

"You don't use this often?"

"I don't." She gingerly sipped from a mug. A second had appeared next to his plate as well.

He had to wonder why. The cold in Arnell wasn't nearly as brutal as in Tuskala, but it was still too chill to forego lighting the hearth most nights.

There were no other, possibly more polite, seating options, but as he moved to sit next to her, she pulled the blanket aside and then tucked it over him, the gesture, once again, shockingly intimate despite the space that remained between them. He eyed the pillow.

"You sleep in here?"

"Ah, ah, you've already asked your question. It's my turn again." She took what he felt was a rather satisfied bite, the drag of her lips as she did so making him wish suddenly, and quite fiercely, that he were a fork.

"I—" He cut off as the realization dawned on him. He'd asked about the fireplace. He let out another deep chuckle. She didn't leap away this time, only burrowed back onto the couch with a smirk. She'd brought her legs up, holding the plate in her lap. He, on the other hand, sat stiffly, nearly swallowed by the sofa, his knees up awkwardly high due to the human-sized furniture.

"What made you come to Arnell? Why not Umbri? Or the Mire Isles?"

"Well, I don't do the ocean, for one. Beside it, sure, sailing over it? Not if my life depended on it. And Umbri is . . . It's drab." He paused, grinning as she snorted. "But I like Arnell. The snow on the mountains reminds me of home. The people are wary, but not hostile, and enough of the obscure races visit or live here as well. Having a traveler's market means there's a chance Tuskalan wares come through. The whole inn is decorated in the style, you should come see it some time."

He shoved a large forkful in his mouth to stop the rambling but groaned in pleasure instead.

"No," he mumbled over the burst of flavor. "You *must* come see it some time. And I must cook for you. There's no way carrying the oil is fair payment for this."

She blushed a pretty pink. "I couldn't bear to trouble you."

"And would it trouble you?" He wouldn't press, but perhaps food was his *love language* as well.

"Not at all," she said. "I'd love to see a little slice of Tuskala. But only if you let me help cook."

The firelight flickered over her skin and danced in her dark eyes, the shadows from earlier banished, especially as she grinned sweetly. "That counted as your question by the way."

5

Elaine

HE LEFT. BUT NOT before securing a promise that she'd stop by the Aspen Inn later in the week. Stock day for the castle tomorrow would mean she'd have a late night, and though the idea didn't seem to bother him, Elaine didn't want to intrude by showing up so soon. She hadn't asked if he lived there, but it seemed likely. What would it be like to live with a rotation of strangers in your home? Certainly chaotic.

Certainly not lonely.

She sighed and sank down on the sofa, pulling her braid apart and tucking the silk under the pillow. The fireplace still burned, the heat making the blanket unnecessary, but she didn't kick it off. It had been too long since she'd been *this* warm. Deliciously, nearly unbearably, warm. Despite feeling her home was left more cavernous in his absence, Elaine smiled.

Then laughed out loud.

The sound didn't echo as his had—but it did smooth something jagged in her, and for some ungodly reason water pooled under her closed eyes. She ignored it, letting the heat lull her to sleep. But, in the night, the fire died, and the house was frigid once more.

The watery gray morning was damp with a low-hanging fog as Elaine walked to the castle. She made it a point to arrive extra early each day, ensuring a smooth start.

The streets weren't empty, since the work of the fishmongers and bakers began early as well. This time was reserved for the laborers, free of the cold regard of nobility—though the working class had its own prejudice, its own hierarchies, of course. That would never change.

Elaine was lucky.

Castle work was coveted: good wages, food provided, even lodgings if one was okay with communal living. Elaine had considered it more than once, but it felt too much like another step backward. If she sold her home, she may be free of the monthly payments that ate up most of her single income, but what would she have then? Nothing. At thirty-four, she was already too old to be childless and unmarried without raising eyebrows. Were she a wealthy woman, none would bat an eye, but life in the city was difficult, sometimes impossible, on a single income, and family values were one of those things the working class clung to more than those who could afford not to.

She plucked a few sprigs of chamomile from the castle's kitchen garden for the morning tea before making her way inside and filling the kettle up as high as it would go; her team would be here soon.

The pantry's sparse offerings meant stock day had come in the nick of time. She'd been ordering extra, but none had expected Corsair to stay this long. Nor had any expected the princess to disappear, or the manhunt that followed.

The rumor was she'd been kidnapped by Umbri's scoutmaster—the Wingbreaker himself—and outwardly, this seemed to be the case. Wanted posters and public service announcements meant every person in Arnell knew to be on the lookout for the fiery princess with long red hair, but whispers among the service staff claimed the king didn't worry for her safety. In fact, he seemed angry with her, of all things.

Elaine's gut churned. She sipped her tea, hoping the dried peppermint she'd added would calm it down. She should have asked her friend more questions. At the time, it seemed wiser not to know, and while it may still be true, it may also be true that she'd aided the princess into the hands of an enemy spy.

"Morning!" Airam sang, already shedding his cloak.

Elaine jumped, spilling hot tea over the side of her mug.

"Oh, sorry love, shoulda warned ya." He hung his cloak with hers.

"No, it's okay! Good morning. Tea?" Elaine had already poured him a mug as well. As he tied his braids back, she gathered the parchment and ink and, together, and they spent the next half hour finishing up the supply list. Turns out they'd need . . . well . . . everything, but the order went out before the sun was high enough to begin its reach over the castle walls.

After breakfast—mostly pre-made breads and pastries, oatmeal, and a quiche as well since the hens were laying again—Elaine managed the wagons that rolled in with the restock. Airam and Roman ferried in sacks of flour as the tradesmen unloaded, and she quickly scooped up any delicate glass bottles. She was tucking them in the highest cabinet when the kitchen doors quietly opened.

Dread drained the blood from her face, forcing it to her quickening heart.

"Elaine, right?" The lord let the door swing close behind him.

Elaine bowed. "Yes, Lord Sebastian, can I get you anything?" The man was actually Prince Dimitri's cousin, royalty in his own right. The two of them, along with their king, initially visited to cement Corsair's alliance with Arnell through an arranged marriage.

The one Elaine had helped the princess flee.

"That won't be necessary."

Her stomach squeezed. He wore a relaxed, disarming expression: lips curled up slightly, kind eyes, hands tucked in the pockets of the black suit he always wore.

The casual posture did nothing to quell sudden nausea. Her heart thundered in her chest. "It's my turn?"

"Yes, Lady Elaine. If you'll follow me."

6

Satyr

"THAT'S NOT THE PRICE we agreed on," Satyr said, his voice low. This side of the square stayed busy, but this contact preferred to meet in the open: plenty of people, central location. They sat nursing tea at The Full Cup, excellent cake rolls. He'd never been able to replicate them. He was a chef—not a baker.

"And yet you'll have a hard time arguing it, won't you?" Chorin replied, with a slimy smile.

The asshole.

Satyr tossed him the coin, overpayment included, and snatched the envelope.

His usual, placating smile was more of a grimace as he made his way back to the inn, and Arnell's citizens gave him a wide berth. It seemed even information had increased in price lately, but knowing the taxmaster's schedule ensured none of the pearls they skimmed were missed. Still, if the margin for smuggling continued to narrow, the inn would be in trouble. It wasn't quite in a place to stand on its own.

On top of that, the orders were getting smaller. His usual buyers were nervous; the kingdom was still crawling with guards after the ordeal with Wolf and the princess.

Gods, he was glad they were okay. When the driver to Lamel mentioned they'd decided to brave the forest rather than sticking to the main road, Satyr wasn't surprised, but he did wonder at the wisdom of dragging the princess into that level of peril. She seemed likely to fall over if faced against a strong wind, and he'd seen the survivor's shock she'd endured when they came to him for help.

No.

A princess and a forest wouldn't mix well at all.

To be fair, many would think the same of an orc and an inn.

"Table two was asking for you," Sybil said as a greeting when he returned.

Sighing, he looked, already knowing what he'd see.

"Evening, Satyr."

"Hey, Jimbe. I've got the rent in the back."

The fae male wore a bright-red, collared jacket over forest-green trousers, and golden hoops in rows along pointed ears. "Let's slow down a minute. Why don't you have a seat, son."

Satyr managed to keep the worry and irritation off his face. Jimbe was about two-and-a-half-hundred years older than him, though it was impossible to tell. An orc's lifespan was similar to a human's, but Satyr, at thirty-five, was no one's 'son.' At least not anymore.

Satyr settled in and the fae sat back against the bench, slinging an arm along the top. With the other hand, he knocked on the solid wooden table. "I'll be straight with you, Satyr. I'm raising the rent." Satyr tried to interject, to point out that it's not rent if he was buying the place, but Jimbe talked over him. "I know, I know, but tariffs are getting higher, and taxes too."

Satyr folded his arms, unease churning his gut. "What's this really about, Jimbe?"

The male tipped his head sideways, sucking on his teeth. "There are new circumstances. I've had another offer."

"But we had a deal," Satyr growled.

"I'm flexible, son, and I don't want you to go. I just need to ensure I'm getting what this place is worth."

The inn wasn't even profitable, how much more could it be worth? But admitting so wouldn't do Satyr any good. "I could protest this to the estate's offices."

The fae's eyes darkened behind square spectacles. "You could. But a handshake here isn't worth quite as much as where you're from, do you understand?"

Bastard.

Satyr kept his aching fists under the table. The satisfaction he'd get from rearranging the male's face wouldn't be worth having to leave the city. Even if he really, really deserved it.

The handshake deal had been a godsend at the time, no down payment, just taking over the monthly ones. But this wasn't the first time Jimbe had increased the 'rent.' Satyr was supposed to own the place one day, according to their agreement, but the marker kept moving. He should have walked away the first time, or the second, but his heart sank at the real possibility that he may lose the inn, after everything. He bowed his head, deflated.

"Okay."

"Okay?" Jimbe's voice was positively chipper. "Wonderful. The interested party seemed a prudish lot, I much prefer our relaxed relationship. Why don't you rustle us up some food, and then we can iron out the details.

Sybil caught Satyr's eye as he stood, and they each gathered a few empty plates before meeting in the kitchen.

"What'd he want?"

"Don't worry about it, Sybil." Satyr oiled the stone pan. He'd completely forgotten to order the herb infused bottles for the inn. They'd be sold out by now. He slammed the fish down and hacked at it, imagining that he'd taken his broadsword from the wall to wield against his slippery landlord. Sybil scurried away, and guilt edged its way around his frustration. She didn't do well around male aggression, and he *knew* that.

He shouldn't let himself get like this—no matter that he'd never direct it at her. She was too young to be so scared. And if he lost the inn, she'd suffer too.

He topped the fish with a kind of white, sour cheese, and set it in the oven to brown, then took the opportunity to slip into the supply room. From this side, it looked exactly as you'd expect, but clicking open the false wall revealed the hidden space beyond. Like the inn itself, it had two floors. The bottom was shelves, the top held a couple beds and a chest for those who might need a discreet place to stay. Today, it was all but empty—the last shipment was late—but checking confirmed at least he had what Talilah had ordered. With any luck, it would be enough to make up for the increased 'rent.' He carefully clicked the false wall back into place.

He plated the fish and called, *"Fáilte!"* as he walked back through the dining room and more guests came through the front door. "I'll be right with you," he said, then turned and coached himself, again, to remain calm in the face of the unpleasant evening.

"Thank you," Talilah purred, wrapping clawed fingers around the pearls with uncanny grace. The dragonblood was also gifted with horns, lilac skin, and iridescent, patchy scales, but it seemed rude to ask.

It wasn't rare for her to stop by the inn, but she'd asked to meet in a now-familiar darkened alley. He'd often wondered if she lived nearby, but, again, it was none of his business.

Neither was what her employer did with the pearls.

She flashed him a smile full of white fangs. "Have you reconsidered the offer?" she asked, eyeing him like a hunter eyes its prey.

"No need." Satyr kept his tone carefully neutral. It had crossed his mind more than once over the course of the day. A new job might be the solution to his current struggles, but while he'd be happy to give up the smuggling, he loved the inn too much to leave.

She sighed, weighing the bag in a hand. "And this is all you had?" she asked.

He nodded. "For now."

The next shipment was supposed to have been delivered four days ago, and if it didn't show before the end of tomorrow, he'd have to hunt his man down. Like a fool, he'd already paid for it, and it seemed likely they wouldn't make it to next month's 'rent' if he didn't do something soon.

"I'll check in for the rest in a few days," she said casually. "If they're unhappy, it'll be me that suffers for it, you know."

He swallowed as she slinked away.

True nighttime sucked the joy from the streets of Arnell, dampening colors and muting the typical sounds of the city. The ever-present breeze blew forgotten or neglected garbage down the narrow, cobbled street. Satyr bent to retrieve it—stray baking paper. He stuffed it in the next bin he found, offering a small smile to the ragged looking fae woman that gave him the side-eye as he passed.

At home, he counted the gold, though he had no doubt it was all there. Talilah had been a regular customer before Satyr had taken over the business, and had ordered her magical ingredients directly, and always monthly. The pearls were useful in potions or enchantments, acting as magical multipliers, but what manner of magic the woman dabbled in, he couldn't begin to guess.

The crown controlled the movement of the pearls and other magical components, creating false scarcity and hiking up prices. Satyr didn't go on the water himself, merely skimmed from the top with the help of a couple official harvesters that were grandfathered into the business—it was too risky to get caught harvesting without documentation—and ensured a more . . . even . . . distribution to Arnell's interested parties, as well as a few of the outlying towns.

The irony didn't escape him that he'd fled his home under suspicion of sympathizing with pirates, only to inherit a smuggling business in his new life, but he made sure no one got hurt. Though losing contact with one of his men couldn't bode well.

His room was upstairs, the exact same set up as the rooms they rented; more rectangular than narrow, though his had a few personal touches. A shield with his family crest hung over his bed, a bookshelf stacked full with recipes and Tuskalan myths leaned against one wall. He knelt on the mammoth-skin run before the fireplace, striking flint against steel until sparks caught the kindling. As the fire flickered to life he thought, suddenly, of Elaine, a kernel of feeling flickering as the fire grew.

She hadn't stopped by, though the week and its end had come and gone. While some part of him leapt to assume he'd been foolish to think she would visit at all, he remained patiently hopeful.

Usually, he'd think guests would find his room too sparsely furnished, but the empty nature of Elaine's home intrigued him. Left to her in an estate, perhaps? The thick aura of grief had settled in its dim corners, and he hoped a good meal—one she didn't have to cook herself—would offer a spot of light, as she'd done for him.

He shucked off his boots, tossing them into a corner, and aimed his shirt and pants at the wash basket. His sleeping pants had grown admittedly tighter over the last few years. Perhaps too tight, if the straining of the fabric over the back—and over the front—were any indication. He wasn't as finely honed as he used to be. A relatively peaceful existence and too many good meals had seen to the slight softening of his arms and, if he were honest, his belly too. Though he remained fit enough through the manual labor required in running an inn, it didn't quite match up to swinging a broadsword in battle. Either way, he opted out of the sleeping pants, stuffing them back in the drawer. They were a loss, but the fire and the blanket would warm him anyway.

He sighed as a loud thunk sounded from one of the far rooms. He never put anyone right next door to him, but it didn't always make a difference. He'd need to be up early to make breakfast, probably a quiche since the hens were laying again. More than that, he needed to hire someone else, someone who could lighten his load and take over while Sybil recovered from childbirth. She'd insisted, multiple times, that she'd only take a couple days, work with the babe on her back, but Satyr knew she was afraid of losing her place here. He wouldn't allow her to overwork herself. She'd be out for weeks at least, more if the labor went badly.

He sighed again, the sound coming from somewhere deep, likely next to his weary soul. Hiring someone would cost money. Money he wouldn't have even if his shipment arrived.

He'd have to hunt down his contact tomorrow.

7

Elaine

THE FOLDED PARCHMENT TOOK up more than its share
of space. Elaine didn't bother to open it again. She sat,
ignoring the chill of both the tea in her hands and the tears
on her cheeks.

The week after her interrogation was a blur of anxiety.
She all but ran home each evening and spent the mornings
sick with worry that if she went to the castle, she'd be under
suspicion, and if she didn't go, it would be suspicious.
Then, the princess returned, yet the unspoken tension had
only increased, culminating in an uproar in front of the
castle. Elaine had barred the kitchen door and hid in the
storage room with the rest of the kitchen staff, waiting
for hours for the guards to clear the courtyard and set up
even more patrols. They'd never apprehended the magical
attacker, but rumors abounded, each more embellished
than the last.

And then, as suddenly as life had royally imploded, it went on: the delegation from Corsair went home, Prince Callum leapt into renovating the throne room, Princess Madeline ordered no less than two trays worth of sweet pastries a day.

And Elaine's father had died.

For years they'd been asking when he'd retire—he'd been a logger and builder for as long as she'd been alive, but the work wasn't easy on the body. Moreover, it was dangerous. He'd crushed part of his leg once, when a tree fell badly. This time, it seemed fate had other designs. The words on the page lived in her mind now, and she didn't have to see them to hear her mother speak what she'd written too neatly on the tear-stained parchment.

I'm going to stay with your sister. Gods knows she could use the help, and the house—well. It's yours now. It should be plenty of room for you. Middlewood is just as beautiful as Arnell, and work won't be an issue. I know your father would rest easy knowing you were close by. And I would too. I've spent too long trying to be more supportive than selfish, because I didn't want to make things worse. But I regret not saying it now: You've been gone too long. There's no reason to stay in Arnell. I think maybe it's time to come home, Rutabug.

Home.

To a house that had plenty of *room for her*. Just her. Because the single bedroom cottage wasn't suitable for a family of any size.

But her mother was right. There wasn't a reason to stay. Not anymore. To anyone else, the castle job alone would be worth family distance, but the house payment here meant she kept just enough of her wages to get by, and little more. It made sense to go back, but she'd yet to respond to the letter. Logic struggled to sway her resistance to the idea of leaving. To take another step backwards.

But if she'd gone home two years ago, she would have been there for her father. Perhaps she could have convinced him to retire. She could have opened a place there, and maybe he would have agreed to work with her instead. If nothing else, she should have sold this house and stayed somewhere more reasonable, so she could send money back home. *If nothing else,* she should have gone to see them more often, instead of assuming life would pause while she fit herself back together.

Elaine blew out the candle that flickered on the low table and curled into the back of the sofa, balling herself up against the crushing need for change.

It was time to start letting go. Tomorrow she would go to the Estate's Office. The house would need some cleaning, and she'd need to find somewhere to stay until it sold, but once that was done, there were options. She could go to Middlewood.

Stay in the house her father built. Or buy a smaller home, here in Arnell, where she could keep her job and start taking care of her mother the way she should have already. Or perhaps she'd go anywhere else. Umbri, the Mire Isles. She'd have enough coin to bring her mother along and still return to a quiet existence with the rest of her family. Maybe that was the best option. To embrace a dividing event between this part of her life and the next.

Cleaning took two days. She opened all the windows and let the wind carry the dust away and dry the tears on her cheeks. By the end, her entire body ached, right down to her weary soul.

The representative at the Estate's Office was kind, with rich brown skin and thin, slightly skewed rectangular glasses. She tried to match his unfailing cheer, but every third sentence she was hit with the recurring realization that she'd never speak with her father again and it was all she could do to sign what she had to and hand over the deed without falling apart in a mess of tears.

As she left, the sunlight warmed her face just a split second before the bitter wind cut through her dress. It seemed the spring had yet to let go as well.

She'd taken off work for bereavement, letting Airam know not to expect her for the last couple days and at least until the following morning. But now that her task was done . . . What would she do with the day? It would take a couple days for them to begin showing the house, but there was no way she was going back to that ghost of a home. She'd scrubbed away every thought and memory that led her to stay. Now that she'd decided to leave it behind, the thought of being there sent a jolt of anxiety to her gut and down to the tips of her toes.

Her legs carried her to the market of their own accord. The crowd was thinner at this time of day, though it still hummed with life and commerce. She wandered the rows of stalls and wagons, some stoutly constructed and earthy colored, others with fabric walls and ribbons to draw the eye.

"Elaine!"

She turned in a daze, not quite able to identify who'd spoken at first.

"I guess the castle called for nearly every oil we brought!" The Umbri merchant's eyes shined over a broad smile.

"Yes," Elaine said, forcing a smile. Perhaps she should have gone home after all.

"We appreciate it. If you happen to see Satyr let him know I held one back for him! And I promise when I return, I'll have more paprika!"

A small spark of warmth flared in her chest and made its way to her cheeks. Satyr. With everything going on, she hadn't had a thought or moment to spare. She should have visited this past weekend. Hopefully he thought she forgot rather than assuming she was uninterested. Of course, she needed to be *uninterested,* now that she was likely leaving Arnell. Still. She'd make up for her lateness with a meal, at the very least.

As the thought settled in her mind, she had another idea— "Gregor? Why don't you let me take it to him now."

8

Satyr

"Failte—?" She paused in the doorway, squeezing her fingers over a familiar glass bottle.

He chuckled to cover the way his heart picked up speed. "*Fáilte. Céad míle fáilte!* The orc's welcome. Because you're here!"

"I'm here," Elaine said as she nodded, easing the door closed with a small smile.

He stood behind the dark wooden counter, trying to kick himself into movement and perhaps more intelligent conversation. "You came."

"Yes. Is . . . is that okay?" She tucked her hair behind an ear. It was long and loose today, falling over her shoulders in wind-tousled waves. There was no sign of the shimmering pink silk that graced her on their first meeting.

"Of course it's okay," Satyr said, scrambling. He'd faced battles that flipped his stomach less than seeing her in his inn, with her nose and cheeks pink with cold. "Don't you have a hat?"

Her hand flew to the top of her head, smoothing it down self-consciously. "Why? Do I need one?" The nearby table of dwarves grinned at their interaction, and a slow flush of red crawled up her neck as she noticed, clearly embarrassed.

Satyr crossed the distance in a few swift strides, putting himself in the way and making sure he had her full attention as he spoke again. "Elaine, your ears are cherry red, and I'm no expert on human ears, but I'm certain they shouldn't be. Please." He gestured to the table nearest the fire. "Sit. Let me get us something warm to drink."

"I brought this," she lifted the oil to him as they walked. "Gregor held it back for you."

He took it gingerly, his lips tugging up on their own. "You didn't have to do that."

"It's the least I could do," she said with a half-smile, mirroring his words from their last meeting.

Once she sat sufficiently close to the fire, he went to put the oil away and warm some milk over the stove top. A tell-tale scent in the air made him check the bread in the stone oven. His nose never led him astray—the loaves were perfectly crispy on the outside, the crust split down the middle where he'd scored it. Really, it should cool before being eaten, as it would continue to cook until it made it to room temperature, but there was something about fresh bread still hot from the oven. He sliced a loaf in half and the half into slices, spooned a few helpings of butter onto the plate, and made sure to grab a spreading knife too. The chocolate was a luxury. Luckily he'd been able to source it in bulk, and only carved slivers of pieces away for special occasions.

This was a special occasion.

It melted into the hot milk with some stirring and he carried everything back into the dining room wearing a broad smile. Sybil gave him an odd look, but he only had eyes for the golden-haired woman who waited for him.

Elaine gasped. "Satyr, is this fresh?"

"Mmmhm," he confirmed, satisfied by the look in her eye.

With delicate fingers she tore a slice in half and tasted it and her appreciative moan had him shifting in his seat.

"I make so much bread in the castle, but I never eat it fresh like this. If I did, the rest of the staff would, and then there wouldn't be any left to serve to the family."

"How long have you worked in the castle?" Satyr asked as he buttered a slice.

"Mmm this is so good too!" she said, distracted by sipping her drink. "I don't use chocolate enough." She cleared her throat. "Mmm, let's see, I started when I was twenty-two, and now I'm thirty-four, so twelve years so far."

"Is it stressful? I bet the head chef in a castle's kitchens is really intense."

"I certainly can be." Her impish grin flipped his heart in his chest and her molten eyes flickered with the fire in the hearth.

Satyr laughed, "Wait, you're the head chef? Actually, I should have known. Now I'll have to try doubly hard to impress you."

Her grin softened. "I doubt that. I got lucky."

"What do you mean? Do your parents work in the kitchens?"

Her smiled faltered for a fraction of a moment. "No, no. But they let me apprentice with a baker since I was old enough to roll dough. I always loved it. So when I moved here, she must have given one glowing recommendation. I was allowed to help out in the castle when they were short staffed. I needed the money at the time. But it wasn't long before they offered me a permanent spot. I could do more than bake by then. I wanted to learn it all. And by the time a new head chef was needed, I suppose I had enough experience. Any of the other, fae cooks could have taken the position, I'm sure. Like I said, I got lucky."

"Bull."

Elaine laughed, indignantly. "I beg your pardon."

"There's no way you"—Satyr raised his hands to quote—"'got lucky.' I'd bet there was quite a stir when a human got the position."

She pursed her lips sideways. "I like to think the king and his family didn't give it a second thought."

"And the other workers in the kitchen? How did they feel?"

She studied the table, one slender finger tracing the pattern of its wood. "Some of them left."

Satyr nodded. It made sense. Fae tended to be . . . particular. Part of living so long, he assumed. He didn't doubt the offense some would take to working under someone so young. Young compared to them, at least.

"So," she went on, too-lightly, "clay cups and plates?"

Satyr brandished his cup dramatically, tilting it into the light. "Why yes, my lady—"

"Elaine."

"Why yes, *Elaine*," Satyr said, feeling heat rush to darken his cheeks with the taste of her name. "It's a nod to Tuskala. Clay and stone are preferred. There's hardly any glass or metalware there, as glass is too delicate, and the metal is better used in forging."

"They're beautiful."

They were, they were thick and carved with intricate patterns. Some were painted with florals or landscapes, though the color had faded with time and use. It didn't bother him, though. He couldn't grasp the concept of owning dishes purely for decoration.

"And those?" she asked, motioning over their heads to the bunched group of flickering orbs.

"Paper lanterns, there are candles inside. We light them every morning." There were individual ones around the room too, of varying sizes. She watched them, and he watched her.

"I'm glad you came," he said, but her return smile was reserved, a line slowly formed between her brows and he fought the urge to smooth it with a finger. "What is it?"

"I hoped that I . . . could rent a room."

Satyr's stomach swirled itself into knots. She wanted to stay here? "In the inn?" he said intelligently.

"If you think it would be too odd, I can stay elsewhere. I don't want you to feel as though we've hardly met and I'm crowding you—I'll be no bother, and I'd make it worth your while." Her cheeks got another shade redder as her eyes widened. "With coin, I mean."

He huffed a laugh, blushing furiously now. "I'm happy to take your money, but if it's just for a few days you can—"

"It would be longer than a few days, I think. I just need—I just need time. To . . ." she trailed off, the cheer he'd already grown used to remarkably absent.

"You don't have to explain." He could feel the scattered thoughts in her as if they were his own. "You can stay as long as you'd like, Elaine. With no expectation from me."

"And I'm paying."

He nodded. "If you insist."

She sipped the hot chocolate, both hands wrapped around the clay mug. "This really is divine. If you don't mind me asking, where do you get your chocolate?"

He knocked on the wood and sat back, happy to accept the sudden subject change if it meant life would return to her eyes.

"From some of the Corsair traders, but the confectioner is rarely here, maybe once a quarter."

"I'll have to try it out next time, our normal shop changed hands and it's too powdery now, and they stopped offering the sweet kinds. Sure, I like to use chocolate to bring out the complexity of a dish, but I also enjoy some good old-fashioned sugar."

Satyr chuckled. "Me too, tomorrow I'll make us a chocolate tart, what time do you expect to be back from the castle?"

She huffed a surprised laugh and studied the table, tucking her long hair back. "It's been a while since I had someone ask me that question."

Satyr wanted her to look at him. He reached an arm to stroke the hand that held the mug, "I'm asking."

She only glanced at him before averting her eyes again, but she rested forward on her elbows and clasped a hand over his.

"Thank you."

His bliss faded with the sadness in her tone. He waited, wanting desperately to press, but she seemed unlikely to explain, and unlikely to appreciate his insistence.

"Usually," she continued, "I'd be home just after the dinner hour, though there are evenings it may be later."

Satyr nodded. "Sybil!" he called, a bit too loudly if the way she jumped was any indication.

Elaine followed his gaze, brow furrowing softly when she noticed the heavily pregnant server hobbling toward them.

"Sybil, this is Elaine, would you mind putting a little tray together for her, I'm going to show her to her room. I'll come back down to get it in a moment—don't try to carry it up the stairs."

Sybil offered a smile to Elaine, rolling her eyes as if to say, "overprotective orcs, huh?" but Elaine only offered a tight smile in return. Satyr extended a hand and pulled the human woman to her feet.

Purposefully, he refused himself the opportunity to study her again, afraid he might scare her away, or make her believe he expected anything untoward as he led her to an empty room. Clay vases wrapped in rope netting were nestled in corners or shelves on the walls. Most were decoration—he couldn't leave anything of value out in the dining area. Despite how prosperous Arnell seemed to be, there would always be thieves.

The stairs creaked their familiar protests as they went up. The top opened to a floor to ceiling tapestry of snowy mountains. They followed the hall around as it turned and lengthened, with dark, wooden doors springing up on either side. The rooms always filled closest to farthest, but if she was staying a while, she'd want to be as far from the noisy patrons as possible.

"This one's mine." He tossed a knuckle into the door of the one farthest down. "And this one"—he inserted the key into the one directly across—"will be yours."

He entered and placed the key on the nightstand. "Not much to show, but I'll bring up some fresh flowers tomorrow.

Any clothes you want washed, you put in the hamper." It was cold, so he grabbed the flint and steel and lit the fireplace. "Did you bring any bags?"

"Not this time, but I will." Her knuckles bone white from the way she clasped her hands in front of her. Her voice was small, her eyes too shiny.

He had no idea what to do, so he stood, lifting his arms, palms up. He tilted his head in a question, and she nodded, her face crumbling as the first tears fell. When she collapsed into him, he couldn't help but notice how velvety soft her body was, or how the brown sugar scent of her wrapped around him, warm and inviting. She shook silently, her hands gripping the front of his tunic. He tried to rein in his questions, to respect that she'd talk when she was ready, or maybe that she'd never explain at all. Still, he couldn't help but wonder why she had an entire, ghostly home all to herself, yet she planned to stay here. Or why she slept on a sofa in a half-empty, frigid room. Or why, of all people, she sought comfort in him.

When she stepped back, her cheeks and nose were as red as they'd been when she walked in. "I'm sorry," she said. "That was horridly inappropriate. I'm not usually like this."

He shook his head. "You—"

"Satyr." Sybil appeared in the doorway. She'd brought the food up anyway, of course. Stubborn young woman. She'd give birth on the inn floor at this rate. He released Elaine and swept the heavy tray from her. "You're done for today, go ahead and sit down somewhere." Sybil gave them both a polite nod before going out, and another door in the hall opened and closed.

"She lives here?" Elaine asked, her voice uncertain.

Satyr sighed. "The babes not mine," he said, as bluntly as possible, so there could be no confusion. "Sybil doesn't have anyone. She . . . needed new people. Someone who would give her work and a roof."

Elaine nodded.

It was still chill in her room. The night seemed unwilling to let go, but she had no bags, nothing but the dress she worked in. "I'm going to go get you some warm night clothes."

He strode to his room and shuffled around for the too small sleeping pants, and the shirt that matched. They'd look like a tent on her, but it was better than being cold. Or rather, he should at least give her the option.

When he returned to her room, he placed the folded clothes on the bed.

"I'm going back down to finish out the night. If you need anything, I'll either be there, or in my room . . . I tend to sleep heavy. If I don't answer, feel free to come poke me." He offered her a smile, hoping the half-joke would lighten the mood.

Her eyes were dry now, but she only pressed her lips together and nodded again.

Back in the dining room, he topped off drinks and took empty plates to the kitchen. There was nothing more he could do to help her, beyond giving her privacy. She had a bed, food, and clothes for the night. What else could he do? A thought dawned on him.

But he'd have to catch her before she left in the morning.

9

Elaine

THE SLEEPWEAR WAS PERFECTLY oversized, and the hearth already had the room warming up. She went to the window, peering past the simple latticework, arms wrapped around herself.

She should have thought it through, should have gone home and packed a bag. She'd considered selling for a long time after she and her partner separated, but hadn't had the heart to. More and more often, she felt she didn't have the heart to face it either, day after day. All she needed was some sense of control, to *do* something. The thought was terrifying. She'd lived in Arnell for over a decade, and as the years went on, she'd visited her family less and less. She could barely make a showing at a holiday without the pitying looks and too-loud whispers.

And then there were the children.

It wasn't that she begrudged her sisters the fact that they could have normal lives. Traditional families. But, after years, the tangible reminder of her infertility meant she always wore a fake smile, and though they asked after her job and praised her talents, it was a poorly applied bandage to the wound in her chest.

She liked to think she was getting better. Becoming okay with the life that she'd lost before it ever existed. It had slipped through her fingers like ocean water, leaving a briny, gritty feeling she couldn't wash away. Maybe if she left Arnell she could start fresh. Leave the house. Leave her old life. Find a new dream. Still, when it came to her father, it was too late.

In the morning, she woke with a start, her heart sinking as she realized she was even in a bed.

But, gods be praised, it wasn't hers.

She tidied and folded her borrowed sleepwear before donning the same dress she'd worn yesterday. It was unfortunate, but it would have to do. Her pulse picked up as she walked down the hall, now able to hear noise from the dining room. The paper lanterns were lit, and the early patrons were quiet, nursing cups of tea in an attempt to prepare for the day.

Of course, Satyr would already be up, tending to the morning labor crowd. She threw a brief glance at the counter, wondering if he'd be there, but it was empty, save for the bottle racks and enormous broadsword that hung on the back wall.

"Elaine."

She turned and came face to face with a massive, green arm. She trailed her eyes up the grooves of fine muscles, finally meeting his smile. This one was real, if she were any judge, and the mischievous glint in his eye let her know he definitely recognized gawking when he saw it.

"No time for breakfast?"

She gave him her best "I'm completely innocent" blink, as if she hadn't ogled him at all, but still failed to fight the edges of her smile down. "I'm afraid not."

"Can you spare a moment?"

Technically, she could spare a few. She was always early to work. She nodded.

"Here, come on."

She followed him to the back, sucking in the smell of bacon, eggs, and biscuits.

But the kitchen was empty.

"Is it just you in here?" she asked, surprised.

"It is. Sybil helps manage the crowd and sometimes pops back here if I need a hand, but for the most part it's just me."

"All day?"

"All day," he agreed, wrapping a bowl of eggs and bacon, and then some biscuits and placing them in a bag. He hesitated before handing it to her, suddenly shy. "I was hoping you'd let me go with you to get some of your things. I'm handy when it comes to moving things around."

Elaine's heart leapt into her throat. She'd been dreading going. What if she went back and changed her mind? Or simply didn't have the strength to go through with it?

"I would really like that," she said earnestly. It would be infinitely better than going alone.

He rewarded her with a smile, and she squeezed one of his giant arms in farewell, trying not to admire them lest she be caught gawking again, but she wouldn't deny they felt incredible under her hands. "I'll be home after the dinner hour. Will that be okay?"

"Perfection." He held her stare, and she looked away to hide her blush.

She wrestled with conflicting emotions the entire walk to the castle, sad and relieved about putting her house up for sale, excited and terrified at the idea of leaving Arnell, pleased and melancholy at Satyr's attention. He was kind hearted—that much was obvious. It remained to be seen if he were just zealously friendly and empathetic, or if he had a real interest in her.

But if she was leaving, it didn't matter either way.

The thought gave her a slight ache. At the very least, they'd have been great friends. She'd tried to befriend the other cooks in the kitchen, really befriend them. And they were—friendly—but, for the most part, uninterested in anything but getting home. She was young of course, and human—while they were all fae. The age gap was quite large, and she could only listen enthusiastically to the conversations about things that happened before she was born.

Before her own mother was born.

She was still the first one there, and, after setting the porridge to cook and unwrapping the breakfast pastries she'd prepped, she sat down to eat her own breakfast.

"Good morning!"

Elain leapt in her seat as Airam strolled in, clearing her throat so as to not die choking on some of the flakey biscuit—they were a bit dry.

"Good morning!" he sang.

Elaine drained her tea to get the bread down. "Morning," she wheezed.

Only the grace of the gods got her through breakfast, and then through lunch. And of course, she couldn't let her mind wander when there was dinner to be served. But reality crashed back in as the kitchen emptied. Isobel looked back and waved, but none of the rest said goodbye, heading out as the unit they'd always been. She sighed. At least she'd have few friends to miss if she left.

Alone, she gathered her cloak and wrapped it around herself, arms heavier than normal. Her whole body felt heavy with exhaustion lately.

As she started her own journey home, she could see them a ways up the way, but didn't bother to hustle this time. Other groups strolled down each side of the street, some cheerier than others. Arnell's buildings and businesses stood two stories tall in a hodgepodge of colors—all pastel shades borrowed from the reef just beyond their shore. She ignored the tantalizing scent of pastries that wafted from more than a few cracked windows.

The inn waited on the same empty road, the door creaked softly, and she breathed deep when she stepped inside, enjoying the rich scent of stew and firewood. A bard strummed his lyre at his place near the fire. Several tables were full, and a few fae near the door nodded as she pulled it closed. Satyr offered her a broad smile. "I thought you'd be back soon. Let me let Sybil know I'm going." He disappeared, and she studied the carefully carved wooden door frame, hoping the rumbling of her stomach wasn't so loud it could be heard over the music.

When he came back, he was free of his apron, and he'd redone the tie in his hair. She smiled to herself as he offered an arm in invitation.

"How was your day?" Elaine asked as they stepped out onto the street. She tried to match his steps, unused to walking with someone so much taller than she. It was a short walk to the square, short enough she wondered why Aspen Inn wasn't at full capacity.

"It was lovely. Though the thought of company helped it along. I was actually wondering if you'd like to grab dinner before we go?" he asked, so hopefully that warmth stirred in her belly.

"I might be leaving Arnell," she blurted, unable to bear the thought of leading him on.

He nodded, his voice rumbling as he spoke, "I see."

Was that all he was going to say?

Selfishly, her spirits sank a little lower. But before she could reexamine their every interaction, he spoke again.

"Where are you going?"

"I haven't quite decided. And I may yet stay. There was a death in the family. It's made me . . . reevaluate some things."

He nodded, likely puzzling together her strange behavior over the last couple days. "Is there any way I might help this reevaluation lean in my favor?" He smiled, playful, but no less sincere.

She wanted to laugh but—"I don't know." Her eyes grew misty with the admission. Only sheer force of will stopped tears from falling again, and with that she was empty of every drop of energy she had for the day.

"Would it be okay if I tried?" His voice was devastatingly soft for such a loud man.

Her head whipped to him, searching for the jest. Cramming the honest, foolish hope down her rapidly tightening throat. If she did decide to leave, it would only make it harder. He didn't understand the scope of the situation. Could she tell him? Her regrets, her father's death? About her separation and why, after over a decade her childhood love had fallen apart? Her gut said he would understand whatever she was willing to give. But her heart wasn't sure she could handle it. Not yet.

"Why don't we start with dinner?" she offered, because what did she have to lose?

If there's anything cooking had taught her, it was to follow her gut.

10

Satyr

HE TOOK HER TO The Saucy Seaside, which, in his opinion, had the best pasta on the square. The inside was dimly lit and already full, many enjoying the low thrumming of the string musicians playing in the corner. A cheery human server led them to a table outside by request. Luckily the crowded market didn't quite spill into the patio space, and the sun warmed them easily, with no wind to undo its work. Just after they ordered, Elaine laid an arm on the table, her eyebrows pulling together as the top wobbled. Satyr pressed a finger down on his side. As he suspected, the legs were uneven.

"Just a moment," he said, unrolling his utensils and folding the cloth napkin in a neat square."

"What are you doing?" She giggled as he dropped to the cobblestone, huffed at the pressure on his stomach, and rolled to his side instead, angling under the table.

"I'm fixing it."

"You're fixing it?"

The legs rocked again as he reached one finger up and pressed the table top from below. "I'm trying to fix it."

Elaine's feet shifted next to him as he folded the napkin once more and wedged it under the wooden leg.

He groaned as he sat up. "That's as good as I can do for now." Elaine leaned to inspect his handiwork as he found refuge in his chair. Like always, he had to keep his long legs out straight under the table, lest his knees tilt it on their own.

She pressed against the table again, grinning. "I can't believe it worked. What made you think of that?"

"Trick of the trade." He returned her smile and felt a rush of satisfaction as her cheeks reddened. She idly fiddled with the ends of the ribbon in her hair and he pretended not to feel the heat from their legs almost-touching.

The silence prompted him to speak again. "I'm very sorry for your loss. I should have said so earlier."

"Ah." She traced a groove in the wooden table. "It's alright. The world doesn't stop for these kinds of things. Even if it feels like they should. It's amazing how many conversations I've had where . . ." She trailed off, her dark eyes round and dark with sudden exhaustion.

"Where it feels like you live in an entirely different world?"

Her eyes flicked back to him, then she leaned back in her chair, tilting her face to the sky. Birds chattered overhead as her chest rose and fell with a focused breath. Perhaps he shouldn't have brought it up again at all, but he felt guilty for being more concerned she'd leave than about what would make her go.

"Is there anything I can do to help?" he asked softly.

"Goodness no." She let her face drop and looked at him. "Truthfully, you're doing so much already. I imagine it's strange to have me as a patron, and stranger still to have things . . . go as they've gone, but know I may yet leave."

It wasn't strange to have her at the inn at all. Satyr was male enough to admit to himself that his heart soared when she showed up. When she hadn't kept their plans to meet the first time, he'd wondered how he could have read her interest so wrong, and been privately worried he might have overstepped a boundary with assumption.

Still, knowing she could leave at any moment meant twin fears—that he'd grow overly fond of her and she'd leave. And that he'd hold back, and she'd leave, with him never knowing what he could have had—no matter how briefly.

"But you're not sure you're leaving either?" It was the most vital piece of information she'd offered.

Their conversation paused as a fae woman with rainbow braids brought their food—long, thin noodles with buttery sauce and slices of roasted chicken. It smelled incredible, and his stomach grumbled in anticipation. As the server poured them a deep-red wine, Elaine studied the meal with interest.

When they were alone again, he spoke. "Do you think that we could . . . enjoy the time we have? I would like to get to know you, while I can. Is that okay? I won't put any pressure on your choice—family is the most important thing to an orc. And I'm not asking for your hand in marriage. I just want to spend time with you until you decide. I want you to teach me how to make biscuits that aren't too dry."

Her fork clinked on her plate as she snorted a surprised laugh and he grinned. Of course she'd noticed. He knew they'd be dry when he wrapped them that morning. Unfortunately, he'd been mother-henning over Sybil when they'd finished cooking and ended up pulling them too late. Of course, he cursed himself for sending her with anything less than a lavish breakfast, and he'd rather have tossed the whole batch, but what he'd rather do was impractical. Speed was vital, as was using all their resources. It wasn't the royal kitchens where you might slow roast a duck for hours, or discard a batch of rolls because they hadn't risen in the right shape. He ran an inn's kitchen well, but it certainly didn't allow for much artistic freedom. Soon, they'd cook together, and he'd take his time impressing her.

She sipped her wine delicately. "The biscuits were lovely," she said, polite, as most of his customers were. Was it because the food met a minimum requirement? Or because he was a seven-foot orc? It was anyone's guess. "And it would be an honor to know you, Satyr."

Her brown eyes were golden in the daylight. His heart flipped in his chest like a freshly caught fish, and he quietly mourned that there would always be a part of him she couldn't know. Knowledge of the smuggling would endanger them both, and at the very least it would risk her job. Not to mention she'd likely bolt out the door if he explained he was a criminal by necessity. She needed to stay at the inn for now, and if she planned to leave, he could make it easier on both of them by sparing her the finer details of his employment.

She'd busied herself with twirling a bit of pasta on her fork. "The king may not mind paprika but I can say for certain he *abhors* capers."

Satyr laughed loud enough to draw the annoyed attention of those around them. Elaine lifted a hand to cover her mouth as she chewed, her eyes twinkling.

His own dish was delicious, but try as he might, he couldn't pull his mind from the troubles that waited for him back at the inn. He was grateful that the payment from Talilah would keep him going for now. Sorting things out for Elaine meant he'd had to put off finding his missing shipment, but he could wait one more day. It wasn't the first time someone had gone off-script and disturbed his system, but when Satyr did find the person responsible, he'd ensure it didn't happen again. He preferred to avoid violence in this part of his life, but a threat to pull the right—or wrong—strings often worked just as well.

"Do you eat here often?" she asked suddenly. He chastised himself for forcing her to keep up their conversation.

"No," he said, determined to push his worries aside. "I reserve this place for the beautiful women in my life, of which there's been very few."

The blush was so easy to see on her creamy white skin, he chuckled. "That one was undeniably cheesy and you're still as red as a tomato."

She scoffed and kicked at him under the table half-heartedly, which only made his own smile wider.

"I imagine you left a few broken hearts in Tuskala when you left," she said.

"Only my mother." He grinned though his heart pinched hard enough he forced the conversation forward. "I was lucky to not be entangled at the time. I always thought I'd settle down after my service, have about a hundred little Satyrs to scramble after, but when it came down to it life went another direction."

"You still have time. Like you said, family is the most important thing," her voice was thin, odd, something too careful in the statement.

He nodded, but she didn't see him, too busy studying her fork as she moved food around her plate. "And how about you?" he asked. "How many broken hearts in your wake? A dozen, two dozen?"

She huffed a laugh, ducking her head. "Only a couple. I was with someone for a long time. But I'm not anymore."

The pieces fell together in his mind. Her house—barren walls, missing furniture. Grief for something gone, one that lived there a long time before the death in her family. "Their loss," he said. Whatever person had left her in such a state was worth less words than that. She chuckled softly. "I mean it, Elaine. I've tasted your cooking." She laughed harder and kicked at him under the table again as he grinned.

When they'd finished, she seemed relaxed, and as they walked, he offered an arm, which she accepted with a smile that made his heart squeeze.

11

Satyr

SATYR TRIED TO DISTRACT her on the way to get her things. The sun still clung to the horizon, and despite his efforts, she was wound back up by the time they faced the familiar door, her steps clipped, her arm unconsciously braced against his own. They went up the three steps to the door and she took a steadying breath. When they stepped in, everything looked exactly as it had before, minus the dust.

She went up the stairs without a word, and he followed, careful to step lightly. It wasn't an old house, by any means, but he'd always worried Arnell wasn't made for creatures his size, and he wasn't certain it was his imagination that gave him the impression the stairs bowed under his weight.

At the top, he found a sitting room on the left side, a door open to a washroom on the right, and two doors farther down, one on either side. He hesitated as she went into one of the bedrooms, deciding he probably shouldn't barge in after her.

On the sitting room wall, two bookcases bracketed a window, but instead of books it held shells of all kinds, the massive ones that children held to their ears, tiny ones with little blue thorns sticking out, twin pink ones with pointed ends. There was a desk, bare, pushed up against the second window that looked out on the street side of the house. A sheet covered a sofa and coffee table in the center.

His ears perked up as he heard Elaine grunt with effort, drawing him to the bedroom to help, but she met him just outside the room with two packed bags. She closed the door behind her, but not before he saw a large bed, also covered with a sheet.

She shrugged a shoulder shyly at the look he gave her, though he wasn't sure what his face looked like at that moment. Hers was wan, as if she'd aged suddenly. The house seemed to suck the light away from her and into its empty spaces.

"May I take those?" he asked, keeping his voice soft so it didn't echo.

"I can manage one." She offered him the second.

He took it easily and looked around. "What next?"

"I think that's it."

He felt his eyebrows pull together as he followed her toward the stairs. "Are you sure?" There was a small chip in the wall of the stairs, as if someone had knocked the furniture on the way up.

"Oh!"

She went down the steps and dropped the bag at the door. He followed her to the kitchen, where she flipped through the seasonings, grabbing the paprika and a couple other bottles. Once that was done, she pulled a wooden stirring spoon off the wall. It was clearly aged, and had a small heart cut out of the handle. "Okay, for now, I'm sure that'll do."

For now. Because later she might be moving everything out and leaving the city for good. He pressed his lips together in a tight line, but was unable to stop the question from spilling out.

"Family heirloom?"

She contemplated a moment. "It was a gift from my sister. She gave it to me years ago, when I first started apprenticing."

By the time they left the house, the stars twinkled overhead, and Elaine's head kept flicking from left to right, peering under her lashes at the strangers they passed. For obvious reasons, Satyr had never had any issue with being out at night, but by the time they reached the main street he'd taken the second bag, braced it in the same hand as the first, and offered her his arm again. She held it with both her hands wrapped over his forearm, and her body brushed his with every step. She leapt straight up when a stray cat darted in their path, and he laughed, earning a scandalized smile.

Elaine huffed a relieved sigh, shaking out her feet as they walked. "I can't wait to sit down. And change into clean clothes! I'm ready to get out of this dress."

"If it gets into the basket, I'll make sure it gets washed."

"Does Sybil do that too?"

"She doesn't"

"You hire a service?"

He huffed a laugh.

"*You* wash the clothes?" she asked in disbelief.

He nodded. "I do. It's always strange when others here are surprised by it. In Tuskala, we learn to do these things from a young age. We believe all tasks are honorable, ever more so if they serve others. No work is above another. Our hierarchies are based on strength, not divided along gender lines or perceived family roles. An orc is just as likely to bash your skull in as they are to offer to wash your bloodied clothes, but they'll do both well—and with pride."

Elaine grinned. "That's certainly different from how I was raised. Humans have always held a belief that worthiness of task equals worthiness of self. It's hard to explain. But if I were to sum it up I'd say there's definitely a hierarchy of work. Worthy work vs dirty work. The fae don't seem to mind so much about the gendered part, but it does seem they have a similar belief."

"It was one of the biggest culture shocks when I got here. That, and the fact that fighting in public is illegal." Satyr lifted his hands to quote. "Disturbing the peace."

Elaine laughed, "I can't imagine you getting into fights often."

"No, not often," Satyr conceded. "Not in public I mean."

She squinted at him, leaning her head against his arm and pursing her lips out in a playful question.

Satyr sighed. "I used to be involved in the brawling rings here."

His heart constricted as her body eased away, until only their arms touched again.

"Oh yeah?" she asked, scanning the opposite side of the small street. "Why's that?"

"It's all I could do, for a while. All I knew how to do. Even giant-kin are more common than orcs here . . . and you have to admit we have a reputation." A reputation for fierce loyalty and pride, a reputation to rip off their shirts and fight anyone who insulted what they held dear. "And Arnell was full of new and hopeful residents, there weren't a lot of jobs to go around at the time."

She was quiet.

"Does that bother you?"

"A little. I hardly really know you. I know that I feel . . . something. I've never been so bold with a male in my life, but I feel like I *know* you—and I don't. Does that make sense?"

His stomach knotted. "It does. I . . . feel something too. And I hope that you can get to know who I am now. And I hope that I can get to know who you are. Now."

She gave him an odd look, brow wrinkled, before fixing her eyes to the road across from them.

"I used to be better."

"What do you mean?"

"I mean . . ." She threw an arm out, but dropped it back down to her side, and sighed. "I used to laugh. I used to think that a beautiful world would welcome me into a beautiful life. I used to be hopeful. A nauseatingly cheery, talented young woman with a bright future, who didn't jump at unexpected noises. I used to love music—sing. Even dance. And now . . ."

"And now?"

She shrugged, the motion as simple as the half smile she gave him. "Now I am this."

All he could see was the pool of stars in her eyes. "What's wrong with this?" he said softly.

She dropped her head away from the look he gave her. Something akin to a laugh escaped her lips as they turned the corner towards the Aspen Inn. The moon was nearly full, casting shadows down the unlit street.

"I love music too," he declared. "And I can't help but sing. I love to cook. And you love to cook. Why don't we cook together, and see if the cooking might lead to the singing? I won't make you join, I'm happy to serenade."

That earned a small smile. "I can think of worse things than being serenaded while cooking."

He ushered her into the inn, and music spilled out as the door opened and closed behind them. There were still a few patrons, half of them enjoying Thorin's song.

"Care to start now?" He winked, and she chuckled. She just needed time. She just needed a place to fall, someone she could trust. A lot of people were like that. It wasn't relegated to a single race—humans, fae, orcs. They all needed a little hope that there was someone out there who might take a second look, try to see past the surface.

"I assume you'd be preparing breakfast for the morning?" she asked.

He nodded. "Every night."

"Well, I'll be right down. As soon as I change."

He carried the bags to her room and dropped them right inside the door, then made a ruckus going down the stairs to ensure she felt she had some privacy. After ensuring there were no spots on the bar in the dining room, he swept the corner where Thorin played, the man too used to his antics to bat an eye as Satyr pulled the broom around him. He took a moment to fluff the mammoth fur on the walls and finally returned to the kitchen to wait. Some strange impulse had him scrubbing at old stains on the wooden counter block. Sybil brought in dishes as the inn slowly emptied, and he scrubbed at them too.

"Alright!" Elaine had donned a clean dress, as simple as the others, but its pale pink hue set her skin to glowing, and she'd braided the silk ribbon into her hair to match. He grinned. "How can I help?"

"If you want to go into the storeroom and grab what we need for cinnamon rolls, that would be wonderful." He indicated to the storage room door and began drying his hands.

When he followed her in, he found her reaching to the top shelf for the flour, wobbling on the very tips of her toes, putting every inch of her shapely form on display. She jumped when he laid a hand at the small of her back and reached over her to get it down.

"Apologies, you'd think they built this room with an orc in mind," he said, handing her the bag.

"I'm tall for a human woman but these shelves are massive—and the trays too!" she exclaimed as she passed into the kitchen. Satyr grabbed the various sugars. Elaine had already found the mixing bowls—a nesting set he'd purchased the first week he'd taken over in the kitchens.

"Any tips?" He smiled at the eyebrow she raised.

"Are you unsatisfied with your current recipe?"

"I'm never unsatisfied when it comes to baked goods."

She hummed, grinning. "My secret is to keep the liquid to flour ratio high. You want the dough sticky, nearly impossible to work with. It's harder to roll it out, yes—but so worth the trouble"

Truth be told, Satyr liked his cinnamon rolls perfectly well, but he was more than a little curious about her process, and the patrons would get their breakfast either way.

He prepared the stone oven while she mixed and brought a pan with tall sides. She gave him an odd look.

"It forces them to rise and be fluffier."

"In that case we must try it!" She smiled, flipping the dough onto the flour-coated counter for kneading. Just then, Thorin stuck up a new song in the dining room.

The water, she sees me
The waves bid me come
Come and then be free
Her beckoning hum

"*Were I to go, I'd never return,*" Satyr sang in a rich baritone, relishing Elaine's laugh, becoming more emboldened by the light in her eyes. "*The water, her song, bid me stay. Stay and don't suffer for absence of land, naught but heartache lay that way.*"

"Do you know this one?" he asked, spreading a miniscule amount of oil over the bottom and sides of the pan.

"Perhaps." She rolled out the dough, correct that it was incredibly sticky, but her patient, diligent hands studiously attended to every snag. Satyr continued singing as he found a knife. "*I knew a girl both witty and fair.*" He tipped a shoulder into her, making her giggle before turning back to the dough. "*Lips pink as rosebuds and black as night hair.*"

She stepped to the side, and leaned her top half over the counter, gazing up at him as she rested her head on one flour-covered hand.

He leaned into the theatrics as she batted her eyelashes, lifting splayed fingers to his chest. "*She said to go, and ne'er return, the heartache, its song bid me stay . . .*"

The song trailed off as he rolled the dough into fat spirals, crowding them together in the pan as he finished each one.

Sybil shouted farewell to patrons in the other room. Heat licked at his fingers as he opened the stone oven and pushed the pan inside. "It won't take too long, nothing worse than a dry cinnamon roll."

Elaine's eyebrows rose, her face mock serious. "I thought you were never unsatisfied with baked goods."

"Ha ha—I'm not. I promise. Not with anyone else's anyway. I'm really looking forward to trying these." They wiped the counter down and stood close as they washed their hands in the sink. The bard continued to sing from the dining area. "What do you think? Should we go and enjoy the music while we wait?"

"Absolutely."

"Wine?" he offered, but she hesitated just long enough for him to change tack. "Hot chocolate?"

She beamed. "Hot chocolate would be lovely."

12

Elaine

HARDLY TWO DAYS INTO their arrangement, it felt completely normal to return to the inn, freshen up, and make her way back downstairs. Elaine looked forward to the cooking and music, and often joined Satyr at the counter to listen to traveler's tales. He had a way of asking questions, polite, genuine, that made complete strangers open up to him. Did he realize that? Working here, he had to see a revolving door of faces, many he'd speak to once and never again. But each was offered his rapt attention. His hand would still, neglecting the cleansing cloth in his hand, and he'd lean against the counter, crossing those massive, green arms, his skin illuminated by the soft glow of paper lanterns, and listen to every word they spoke. It never failed to squeeze her heart, and she marveled at his ability to turn strangers into fast friends. It was the perfect place for him.

"May I take that?" Sybil asked, coming up beside her.

"Oh, let me take it, you've already got all of that," Elaine motioned toward the giant tray Sybil already held. She picked up her plate and followed the woman back to the kitchen.

"Is there anything else I can help with?" Elaine asked, watching her slide the tray by the sink and begin rinsing the dishes. The kitchen was still a mess after the dinner rush, so she picked up a cleaning cloth.

Sybil shook her head but continued to scrub. "Oh it's alright, don't trouble yourself with it. We manage."

"I'm surprised he hasn't hired anyone else." Elaine set a couple dirty pans by the sink. "I assume he plans to?"

"Not that he's told me. Not sure he could afford it, anyhow."

"Well what about when you . . .?" Elaine wasn't sure why it felt taboo to say it out loud. Obviously the girl was going to have the child soon.

Sybil stopped, but she kept her eyes pinned to the dishwater. "I need this job," she said, her voice tight.

"No—yes! Of course you do. He wouldn't replace you." But Sybil still looked uneasy, and after a moment she began enthusiastically scrubbing the counter.

Elaine's stomach soured as she wiped flour off the counter and into her hands, resisting the urge to look over her shoulder as more dishes splashed into the water. "If you need anything, Sybil. If there's anything I can do . . ."

"There isn't."

Elaine nodded and finished wiping, taking that as her cue to leave. Sybil had the help she needed. And surely she had a plan, beyond working in the inn. There were temples here, who helped women and children in these situations, but the inn was preferable, no doubt. It was a good place for her, for now.

When Elaine made it back from the kitchen, Satyr had moved to a booth and sat across from a hooded figure what kept nodding their head. Satyr noticed her and offered a half smile, but she was distracted by a fae with milky grey skin that had just walked through the door. He was dressed in the bright colors typical of Arnell, but Elaine couldn't remember ever seeing a silk elf who lived in the city. He caught her surprise, his smile faltering as she drew in a short gasp at the huge, dark expanse of his eyes that captured the light and almost seemed to glow. A muscle feathered in his jaw as he moved past her to sit at the counter.

Oh gods. She hadn't meant to cause offense. She truly hadn't. She'd been surprised, yes. Maybe a little frightened, just for a moment. Stories of the silk fae painted them as reclusive cave dwellers. Often, they stayed in the mountains, tending to the memory-eating spiders that created their precious silk. She glanced at Satyr again, but he was deep in conversation—were they exchanging coins? The door opened again and another customer walked past her. The silk fae man tapped his finger impatiently on the counter, the tip of one polished black boot bouncing in time.

Elaine went to the kitchen.

She filled a stein until froth spilt over its edge and grabbed the last chocolate tart Satyr had made for dessert.

The orc nearly knocked her over in the doorway.

"Oh, having a snack?" He grinned.

"No . . . it's not for me . . . I—" she stopped.

He watched her, a line forming between his brows.

"I was rude to a customer."

"You? Were rude? To a customer?" The words came out slowly, like he couldn't quite string them in a continuous line.

"Yes. I gasped when he looked at me."

"Should I be jealous?" The question and his grin sent her stomach flipping all over itself.

"No" she laughed, as heat rose into her cheeks. "I—I think he noticed that I was . . . surprised."

"So he gets free ale and dessert?"

Her face lit up in a flame of heat. "Is that okay?"

He studied her for a moment. "Yeah. That's okay, Elaine. Please. My inn is yours."

Awkward silence stood between them.

"Then I should . . ."

"Oh I am standing right *in* your way I'm so sorry."

Elaine exited and slapped the offerings in front of the man. "I'm certain you've heard this before, but you have the most striking eyes."

His thin brow furrowed. "What?"

She floundered, but Satyr swept right up behind her, swinging one giant arm over her shoulders. His body pressed into hers, and the sudden warmth sent a thrill down her spine. The touch steadied her in an instant. "She thinks your eyes are eerie and beautiful and vast, Kelre. Like the ocean on a windless, moonless night."

"Ah," the man chuffed, his milky skin darkening in patches of subtle blue over his cheeks. "I've heard they're eerie for sure. But thanks."

"So"—Satyr unhooked his arm from around Elaine and nudged the ale and tart to him across the bar—"is your mom doing any better?"

"She is." Kelre's already wide eyes becoming ever wider at the offering. "But the venom is powerful. It takes a while for the body to recover even when the antidote is given in time."

"It's not usual for them to attack, is it?"

He'd picked up the fork, but let it tap back down on the clay. "No. But this was a hatchling, though it's rare no matter what. She will be in bed for a couple more weeks."

"The spiders?" Elaine wasn't sure she wanted to ask, but the words popped right out of her mouth, and she flushed as Kelre turned his midnight eyes back to her. They truly were like the vast expanse of a still, dark sea.

"Yes. Those that made the silk in your hair."

Elaine nodded, resisting the urge to bring a hand over the fabric. The silk was renowned, and the spiders too, though she'd never realized—"They're dangerous?"

He scooped a spoon of cake into his mouth and chewed thoughtfully for a moment. "The entire world Atlas left us is dangerous. The creatures are ancient, but with the right agreements—and hundreds of years—have come to trust our people. There is not often trouble, but something has them restless. Even the more civilized spiders are disturbed, though they cannot put words to their fear. I left a long time ago, but my family said there's been rumors about the new aggression. And some of the spiders have gone missing."

"Stolen?" Satyr asked. "For the silk?"

Kelre shrugged. "Hard to say. Neither of our kind can afford for much to change. They rely on our elderly, feasting on their memories." Elaine's face scrunched up before she could stop it and the man snorted. "It sounds horrid I know, but it's not so bad. Just how things are in Dagada."

Satyr turned to grab more steins to polish. "Will you visit your mother?"

As Satyr and Kelre continued, Elaine watched a human man—more finely dressed than the usual customer—walk in and seat himself at the hooded-figure's table. The two spoke briefly, and a bag was exchanged, again, before they each got up and left, one just after the other.

A little knot of uncertainty planted itself firmly in her mind, but it was silly. What could she possibly have to worry about? Satyr ordering supplies?

"Please excuse me," Elaine said to Kelre, who nodded farewell, hardly missing a beat as he explained to Satyr why his third cousin might resort to murder if she saw him visiting in the silk mountains.

Elaine walked into the kitchen innocently enough, but swiveled her head around once inside, ensuring no one was there to watch her sneak out the back door.

Circling around to the front, she waited, pretending to peruse the trinket store window. The hooded figure stalked up the street, deeper into the city. She followed, breath coming out in puffy white clouds. All the while, she berated herself for her madness. So, what? Satyr had an odd way of ordering supplies? Perhaps he'd decided to hire more workers afterall, and they'd be back later, and she'd be feeling foolish.

One way or the other, it wasn't any of her business. She likely wouldn't even be in Arnell long enough for it to matter. Satyr deserved privacy, not to be under suspicion by those he helped. Yet, inexplicably, Elaine's fear pushed her forward. Could he still involved in the underground brawling? Or gambling? Or any other number of habits that might cause the kind of debt that stopped him from having the funds to hire more help? What if he sold illicit substances, or had a problem himself? No, the thought was unreasonable. She'd no doubt recognize the side effects of sun-slug mucus—which offered hallucinogenic bliss and a debilitating crash that lasted for days. And he hadn't pressed her about drinking wine—he hadn't even questioned her hesitation.

They were on the sea-side of the city now, passing signs carved with shop names like "Braver Bait," and "The Ship's Right." Waves crashed along the docks either behind this row of buildings or the next and before too long, the figure took a right turn, headed further towards the fish scented air.

Just as she went to follow, the tips of her toes slammed into a poorly placed stone and its chiseled edge bit through her thin shoes. She sucked in a breath and the hooded figure turned, just enough that Elaine was able to catch a glimpse of her face: lilac skin, full lips, startlingly intense eyes. Elaine knelt, turning her face away and making a show of rubbing her foot. By the time she peered up from under her lashes, the woman was gone. Heart racing, Elaine turned the way she'd come, cursing her curiosity, wondering what had possessed her, and what reason exactly had her stalking a woman in the middle of the daylight. Satyr was good. He radiated it.

He was happy, and sweet, and welcoming, and he'd sung for her. One of her favorite songs—even if he hadn't known how perfect the moment really was or how her body wanted that voice to sink into every inch of her.

Maybe he was involved in something. Maybe she was a fool. But the answer wouldn't matter so long as she had yet to choose to stay. Or leave.

"Hey!" Satyr was rolling dough when she came back into the kitchen "You disappeared on me! Kelre isn't nearly as laconic as he seems, that man can *talk*."

"Just popped out to cool off," Elaine said, trying to hide how out of breath she was.

He looked back at her. "Are you doing okay?"

"Maybe a bit shaky." There was no use trying to hide that.

He gestured to the pot on the stove. "Hungry?"

She huffed a laugh. "No. I'm alright." The crease in his brow made her cheeks burn in shame at the lie. "I think I'll just go lie down for a bit."

"Of course," he said slowly, his too-discerning eyes roaming her for signs of issue. "If you need anything at all, you know where to find me."

She didn't have any other pajamas.

At least, that's what she told herself.

He'd put a tall mirror in her room—a simple, skinny one that leaned against the wall, and she peered in it now, enjoying the brush of satisfaction at how she looked in what were obviously his clothes. She'd never been slender. It seemed her whole life she'd been tall, with a bosom large enough to cause an aching back, a squishy tummy, and wide hips that fell into strong thighs. There wasn't a place on her that didn't rub together or bounce when she walked. Curvy and luxurious. She'd never quite fit in her last partner's clothes, and feeling cozy in Satyr's was a novel comfort.

Her hands were gentle while unraveling the braid. The silk wouldn't likely fray with normal use, but it wasn't worth risking. Her blonde hair fell loose down to her navel. A knock on the door made her jump, and she must have made some sound, because Satyr, from the other side, yelled, "Sorry!"

"Oh! Um. Hi!" she called through the door.

"I've brought you some food."

She was quite hungry, but she couldn't let him see her with his pajamas on, could she? Not when she had a whole bag of clothes here that she hadn't opened.

"Oh. Thank you!" Elaine chirped.

She stood for a moment, hoping to hear the sound of a tray hitting the floor. But it was all expectant silence.

With a sigh, she resigned herself to opening it for him, face growing hotter with every step.

When she did, his eyes immediately flicked over her, and she knew she must be red all the way to the tips of her ears.

"Hey," he said, the green of his face darkening. Was he blushing? Secondhand embarrassment?

"Hey." She grabbed one arm with the hand of another and stepped out of the way so he could walk in, uncertain about taking the unwieldy tray.

"I just thought it wouldn't hurt to bring something up, in case you didn't eat on your way here."

The fish and seared vegetables smelled amazing, and Elaine felt silly she'd fled to her room as if she'd get in trouble for sneaking out.

"Thank you."

He nodded, and went to her fireplace without a word, and lit it.

"Feel free to let me know if you need anything else," he said.

The formality disappointed her for some reason, but as he left, he stopped.

"You can keep those . . . by the way," he murmured, over his shoulder, as if worried she'd spook if he spoke too loudly.

The door closed with a soft snick.

She beamed as she finished the food, regretting that it would be much too awkward to go back down now. *Did* she need anything? The thought of having him back up to her rooms was only just balanced by the concern of appearing needy or inconsiderate of his time. As she settled in for an early night, the worry crept back in. She could just ask him about the hooded woman. Ask him if he was involved in anything untoward. Satyr was genuine, almost raw. She'd never met anyone who wore their heart on their sleeve the same way.

Deep down she knew if she asked, he would tell her the truth.

13

Satyr

IT WAS WELL AFTER dark by the time Satyr slipped out the back door of the inn. He'd gotten word from Lemch an hour ago, but had to make sure the inn was settled before leaving for the night.

The address was for a decent part of town, not that he could see much of it in the dark. Regardless of what people thought, orcs didn't have exceptional vision like the stories claimed. It was as good as the average human's but not nearly as impressive as that of the fae who were born with that particular gift.

The houses here were quite similar to Elaine's—though these were grander and on the port side of town. Tall, narrow, squeezed together with arched doors, flowers hanging off the windows, some whimsical ivy trailing up to the second-story balconies that cradled potted plants and painted chairs. In the daylight this road would be filled with playing children, and the balconies studded with their chattering caregivers. Some might play instruments. Some might bring soft rocks from the beach to draw on the cobblestones, though every attempt would be washed away with the next rain. These were spaces for those that made a living from their work. Modest, but cheerful. The address he found was no different.

He knocked.

"Hello?" The boy who answered the door was young, maybe fourteen.

"Pardon the time." Satyr dipped his head. "Is Beron here?"

The boy's eyes hardened. "No."

"Do you know where I might find him?"

"In the castle dungeon, about to be hanged."

Satyrs stomach fell through the floor. "For what?"

"For skimming his harvest. Selling it to pay for this house and gods knows what else." The young man's eyes were hateful, his nose wrinkled in distaste. His ash colored hair was disheveled, but his fists were clenched, bloodless white.

"No." Nothing good would come from the truth.

"Well neither did we. Now, if you're not here for my sister, I'll ask ya to leave."

"Your sister? Does she need something?"

The boy glared.

Satyr pressed. "I may be able to help."

"I don't need your help." The door slammed, leaving Satyr wondering if he'd played the main role in making him a future orphan.

Satyr sent a messenger at sunrise, just after sending Elaine to work with her breakfast. He could hardly afford the bribe by now, but if Beron was really to be hanged, Satyr felt he ought to know. The man had worked as a smuggler since well before Satyr had taken over. There'd never been a problem before.

What had happened? The worry plagued him through his morning and most of the afternoon too. The message returned just before the dinner rush.

Smuggling charges. They'll hang him within the week.

That evening, he knew Elaine could tell something was wrong. She breezed through the door, but after she'd gone up to change, she brushed her soft hand over his forearm and cocked her head, the ends of the silk dangling down to her waist. She rarely wore it to the castle—might get ruined while cooking. But she always braided it back in when she returned, and he'd begun to think of her as two different versions of herself. Before she left in the mornings, she was frazzled, always in a hurry. When she returned, she was subdued, but it was less exhaustion and more ease.

Now, she pinned him with a curious melancholy. "What is it?"

"Nothing." He shook his head. The stove top was covered in speckles of grease, and he wiped it down, trying not to think about Beron. But she seemed dejected by his answer, so he caught her hand as she pulled away. "I have a friend," he said softly. "He's gotten into a spot of trouble I'm not sure he will make it out of."

"Is there anything we can do?"

"I'm going to do what I can. But now that I have you here, what do you suppose we should make for breakfast?" He forced cheer into his voice.

Elaine laughed. "It's your inn!"

Satyr grabbed her hand, finding himself in need of grounding. She squeezed, and he pressed a soft kiss to her knuckles. "If there's only so long you'll be here, then I want every moment to be yours."

She blushed and beamed, ducking her head in embarrassment, but she still answered, "Perhaps something less sweet tonight? Croissants? Sausage rolls?"

"I like the way you think." He winked.

Her blush deepened to crimson, and he had a sudden urge to feel its heat under his lips.

"Sybil," he called instead, moving to the dining room. "Do you have this?"

Sybil nodded and Satyr followed Elaine into the kitchen. She opened the storage room as if she'd done it a thousand times before, this time able to get the flour from its new, lower place on the shelf.

As she assembled the ingredients, he found the bowls, measuring the flour, salt, and water. *"I knew a girl that was witty and fair.*" Her smile blossomed as he sang again. "*Lips pink as rosebuds, black as night hair.*" He paused, lifting an eyebrow in a challenge. If she didn't sing, he'd continue, but he wanted her to have the opportunity, at least.

She clamped her lips down for a moment shaking her head back and forth, but her eyes were bright enough to take his breath away. Just as he opened his mouth, her high vibrato filled the space. "*She said to go, and ne'er return.*"

He held his hands out. "Yes!"

She glanced away, smiling as she continued. "*The heartache its song bid me stay.*"

He joined so they sang together. "*But stay and I'll suffer the absence of her—when she's but an arm's length away.*"

He scooped an arm around her waist. She fit so perfectly against him. "I don't want to suffer in the absence of you, Elaine. Not if you're here."

She looked up at him from under heavy lashes, one hand rested on his chest, the other slipping slowly behind his neck in a silent question.

"I'd very much like to kiss you now, Elaine," he said, his voice more even than he would have expected from the pounding ache in his chest.

"I'd very much like it if you kissed me, Sa—"

He brought his mouth down to meet the words and slipped a hand around the back of her head, tilting her up to allow for better access. She moaned. *Actually moaned* into his mouth, and wrapped both arms around his neck, the soft cotton of her dress grazing his skin as she rose on the tips of her toes. A lightning bolt of surprise speared through him as she teased her tongue over his lips, beckoning him to open. He pulled her in tighter and gave into the request with glee, relishing her boldness, her need.

The taste of her.

Orcs didn't usually kiss using their tongues like humans, too much complication with the tusks beyond a peck on the lips, but he found himself enthralled by the sensation, the way she flicked it over his lips before slowly dipping into his mouth, languidly exploring. When he pulled away, she leaned forward, eyes half closed, still caught in the moment. Arms still wrapped tight, he nuzzled his forehead to hers. This was the way orcs naturally showed affection, and as much as the kiss sent his blood roaring to places she could certainly feel now, this was a fist squeezing over his heart.

"Thank you."

She huffed a laugh, and he grinned too—like the fool that he was—but he could enjoy this now. He wouldn't let the thought of her leaving spoil this moment. He could dive into melancholy when it was over.

"Oh, sorry." Sybil squeaked, walking through the kitchen door and immediately backpedaling. Elaine pushed out of his arms as Sybil walked back in. "Actually . . . I just have to get . . ." The woman hobbled to the counter quickly—she really was due any moment now. "These." She grabbed both pitchers of ice water and retreated once again.

Elaine tucked hair around both of her ears and hugged her arms over herself, giving him a self-conscious smile.

He returned to mixing, but she hesitated, watching him for a moment. "I wanted to ask you—"

Something colossal crashed in the dining room. "Satyr!" Sybil's voice was high and panicked.

Elaine beat him through the door.

14

Elaine

Sybil braced herself against a table, face contorted in pain. Shattered clay and bits of food littered the ground beneath her feet. Those in the dining room were frozen in shock.

"I've got you." Satyr picked up the woman with ease, and Elaine followed him up the stairs to her room.

"I—I think I'm fine. It's gone now," she said, as Satyr gently laid her onto the mattress. "Sometimes they take me by surprise."

Satyr's brow furrowed. "This has happened before?"

She nodded. "My aunt had a lot of false labor."

"Where is your aunt now?" Elaine asked, tugging and tucking the covers around the young woman. "You don't feel any wetness, do you?"

Sybil shook her head. "My aunt is in Corsair where I left her."

Elaine shot a look at Satyr, and he knew exactly why. Corsair was human-centric, and, if she had to put it bluntly, the majority there seemed hateful of non-human races. Sure, they did well masquerading as a tentative ally for the sake of trades, and there hadn't been any outright hostility since the great war, but there was no denying the royal family kept their human line as pure as possible, and that bled into the attitudes of their people.

Satyr's voice was gentle. "Should we send for her?"

"No." Sybirl spoke the word through clenched teeth, a hand clasped over her swollen belly.

"Are you sure this is false labor?" Elaine asked.

"No," she hissed.

"I'll call for a healer," Satyr said.

"And I'll go get you some water." Elaine moved to the doorway, Sybil nodded.

Satyr announced they were closing early and soon the dining room was empty but for the half-finished meals and empty tankards the few patrons had left behind. He went out the front door and Elaine went to the kitchen, filled a glass, and didn't give the mess on the floor a second look as she walked past. The labor wouldn't progress so quickly that she'd have to deliver the babe, but still her heart beat her chest like a drum. It wouldn't take long for the healer to get here, right? They weren't even sure if it *was* labor at this point. Either way, she took the creaking stairs two at a time.

"Here," she said gently, placing the clay cup on the nightstand. The layout was the reflection of hers, with the addition of a tall mirror and a low bookshelf. Bright clothes burst out of a chest at the foot of the bed, though Elaine supposed her viable options would be a bit more limited now. A small box sat in the corner, with a stuffed creature resting atop it. "Is there anything I can get you?"

The blankets were piled at the foot of the bed. Sybil's face was waxy, her forehead beaded with sweat. "No."

"Are you sure you don't want to send for your aunt?"

Sybil closed her eyes as she spoke. "She doesn't know."

"She doesn't know, what? That you're pregnant?" Elaine said in alarm.

The young woman shook her head.

"She would want to know, wouldn't she? She could help you with . . . all this?" What family would leave a young woman alone, surviving on the goodwill of strangers?

"The father," Sybil's voice cracked, "he's a fae."

Elaine tried to reign in the questions. It wasn't any of her business. Clearly the father either didn't know or didn't want to be involved, and the window to end the pregnancy with magic had long since passed. Truly, it didn't matter how either of them had gotten to this moment, Sybil needed to keep her focus moving forward. Perhaps the only thing they truly had in common.

A slow tear leaked from the corner of the woman's eye. "I don't know if I'm ready for any of this."

Elaine sucked in a breath, at a loss for what to say. She waited with the woman as her breath became more even and her body relaxed.

Soon enough, Satyr knocked and didn't wait for a reply before opening the door. "The healer is here."

"Well send him away. I can't afford to be seen." Sybil sighed. "And it's all but stopped now."

He crossed his arms. It was incredibly distracting. "We'll find a way to manage the damn fee, Sybil. You're being seen"

"You can barely pay my wages," the young woman scoffed. "Don't even try to deny it."

Satyr's face hardened, a look Elaine had never seen before. "You're being seen."

It was clear Satyr would rather toss the coin for the next restock than let Sybil go without. Elaine had to agree. There were too many possible complications, and no price was too high for peace of mind—if you were one of those privileged enough to be able to afford it.

"I will pay for the healer," Elaine declared as she marched out the door.

The man in the hallway wore tiny spectacles and held a strange tool around his neck that was shaped like a funnel on either end, one smaller than the other. A wet blotch of dark red marred his shirt, as if he'd spilled his drink.

"She's a non-citizen. Mark the fee down to Elaine Galliade, please. I'm the castle's head chef. It'll be settled in the morning. She bristled as the man looked her up and down, as if, if she didn't pay, it would come out of his wages personally—but all fae with the ability to heal were employed by the crown, and though they didn't have the option of choosing their profession, they were guaranteed regular wages.

His voice was even, almost bored as he tucked dark, mid-length hair behind his slightly pointed ears. "You realize if you don't pay she's the one who will serve time?"

Elaine huffed at the wasted time and crossed the hall to her rooms, only to grab the coin purse from her things and toss it at the man, who fumbled to catch it and awarded her with a glower.

"Consider this a down payment," she said, voice as tight as her shoulders. "I'll remind you she may have a child at any moment so if you don't mind, stop standing around like a useless cockatrice and make sure she's alright."

Satyr gawked as the healer squared his shoulders and walked into the room. Elaine blushed.

"*Please*," she called after the man, clearing her throat.

"We will need privacy," the healer insisted as Satyr and Elaine crowded the doorway.

Satyr spoke slowly. "Sybil. Is that okay with you?"

Sybil hesitated.

"I'm going to have to do a very private exam," the man reminded her, his voice gentler than it was.

"Would you prefer we find a woman healer?" Elaine asked, watching the healer nod thoughtfully, though he said nothing.

Satyr shook his head. "I should have ask—"

"No no, it's fine," Sybil said. "A healer is a healer, you go on."

"I'll be right outside," Satyr's voice rumbled so low with the threat that Elaine grinned despite his stony expression.

Sybil's eyes flicked to Elaine, her mouth twitching up too. They backed into the hall. The door moved on quiet hinges, the soft snick as it closed sealing them both in silence as they strained to hear if anything was amiss. After a while, it flew open again, and Elaine skittered back from where she'd been listening by the door.

"It was false labor," the man declared, not breaking his stride as he moved down the hallway to leave.

Elaine followed on his heels. "Well, how can you tell? You can't have been in there more than a quarter of an hour."

The man whirled. "She isn't dilated. Her waters aren't broken. It's stopped. And there's been no other signs. Her family has a history of false labor, now either you trust me to do my job, or you want to pay me for more of my time—but she's not having that baby right now.

Satyr put a hand on her shoulder. "She's gonna be okay," he whispered softly.

"And you"—the man's eyes went to the orc that stood behind her—"try speaking in a civilized tone, next time, I thought the guards would lock you up for the way you were raving. It does more harm than good."

Elaine lunged for the man as he turned away, but Satyr gripped hooked an arm around her and turned her into his chest, squeezing until the only thought left was of the pressure and delicious warmth of his strong body. He spoke into her ear as the man's footsteps retreated and she could hear the grin, "He has a point. I'm sure half the market thought there'd been a murder."

She laughed, the kind that was on the verge of crying, and his body shook as he tried and failed to hold back his own chuckle. The sound rumbled through her, further grounding them together. He pressed his forehead to hers.

"He is an ass though," he said, still grinning.

"My thoughts exactly." Elaine took a breath relishing the feel of him before she pulled back. "We should check on her. Get her something to eat."

"Agreed."

Sybil was insistent on getting back to work in the morning, though Satyr was equally insistent she not carry a thing. Elaine smiled at the memory as she walked to the castle. When Airam greeted her with his usual singing, she didn't flinch, too busy enjoying the breakfast she'd helped make the night before.

"*Good morning!*"

"Good morning, Airam. I hope you're well."

"Oh, I'm great," he said as he hung his cloak. "The husband's taking me out tonight. I cannot wait to eat somebody else's cooking." She laughed, and he regarded her for a moment. "I wanted to ask—Are *you* doing well?"

Elaine hesitated. "Yes, what makes you ask?"

He shrugged, grabbed a pan, and shucked a dollop of butter. "You just seem distant lately. I'm not the only one who's noticed you're leaving earlier and earlier during the day. The same thing happened when . . ."

When everything had fallen apart. She'd been a mess for at least a month after Seymour had gone that last time—late to work, sobbing in the pantry. A decade of life had just up and left. Airam had covered for her, had all but begged her to take time off. But she wasn't going to explain her father's death to him. She wasn't ready to tell anyone in the kitchens that she may be leaving. "No. Nothing happened . . . I'm selling my house."

"Oh! Good for you! It's about time—what?" His eyebrows rose as she pressed her lips together. "I only mean that it's been a long time coming."

She was annoyed that the man was right, and that it took such a drastic push to do what so obviously needed doing. Her heart sank. The kiss with Satyr was suddenly bittersweet. He knew she may go, but still he offered his time, his affection. Was it wrong for her to accept? She'd already taken such advantage of his kindness. The odd interaction in the inn plagued her mind again, the secretive woman, his mention of a friend in trouble. It all jumbled to form a familiar twisting in her gut. She didn't know him. Not really. And he found it easy to like her now, but he didn't know her completely either. She wasn't so foolish as to assume he'd brush off the sacrifices that came with loving her.

Not that he *loved* her.

She'd been away from any kind of affection for so long her mind was making unreasonable leaps. This wasn't a big deal. Some fun, some laughs.

He knew she was leaving.

She hadn't needed her cloak this morning because it was so warm, but with night came a chill wind that bit at her bare arms and whipped her braid as she walked. All the same, she needed to stop at the post office and send a letter to her mother. The thought made her stomach flip. She'd had no idea what to say.

"The house is up for sale but I've yet to decide if I'll come home?"

"As much as I cannot stay here, I can neither go back?"

"I'm sorry I wasn't there when you buried him?"

"I'm sorry I wasn't there"

"I'm sorry"

Perhaps she should weep on the parchment and send it alone.

The post office was on the main road, arranged in a pale-orange, weatherbeaten building with wide windows. In the end, she sat at one of three miniscule tables near a roaring fire. The letter was haphazard, less than eloquent. She made it clear that circumstances had given her the push she needed to sell the house, but that there were affairs yet unresolved in Arnell, and she couldn't make any decisions yet. And, of course, asked her mother to tell her father, next time she visited where he lay, that she loved him bigger than the star-dusted sky.

Once it was settled, she continued the inn, wiping her eyes and doing her best not to draw any undue attention. When she walked in, Satyr met her at the door, embracing her so hard she squeaked under the pressure. She let herself absorb the touch, swallowing down more tears. She'd gone too long without this kind of comfort. It seemed she cried every time.

"You must be starving," he said, his voice rumbling down to her bones.

She cleared her throat. "My stomach isn't feeling quite right, actually. Where's Sybil?"

"Resting in her rooms if there's any mercy in this world."

Elaine huffed a laugh, and he grinned, pressing his forehead into hers.

"Your dining room is a disaster," she murmured.

"My mind has been occupied."

She could feel herself blush as he spoke, the mingling of their breath feeling more intimate than any kiss. "I had a few stops to make," she said, pulling away.

He watched her for a moment, and she considered saying more. Or perhaps asking about the woman she'd followed, but it seemed trivial now. Even if he was into something untoward he'd been nothing but kind and generous to her. She had far more important matters to be concerned with. There was no point in off-loading her insecurities onto him, complicating things with her unfounded suspicions. He offered a soft smile that shined in his eyes, but the sudden warmth she felt in return was tempered by a nagging and increasing ache that had made its home, long ago, deep in her chest.

15

Satyr

SHAME AND DESPERATION SENT Satyr to the docks in the dead of night. He needed to get the missing pearls at whatever cost. He couldn't let Elaine pay for the healer again. So, he left long after she and Sybil had gone to sleep. A strong, frigid wind meant the sea crashed in with a briny spray, jostling the ships tied to the piers, but he needed no cloak. His body was built for the ice of Tuskala. He'd been to the holding warehouse once before, when he'd first taken over the smuggling, but usually the pearls were delivered to the inn inside the fish he ordered.

The building was three stories tall, red brick on the bottom with white trimmed windows, but the top two floors were solid, dark wood, with a staircase on the side going up. Breaking in would be a hefty crime. All the warehouses belonged to the crown, and tradesmen used them for a fee of their profit. Those he paid to skim their pearl harvest were supposed to drop a pearl-stuffed fish at the holding spot for each run, if they could spare it without suspicion. The process was simple enough—pop the component into the mouth of their most recent capture, and mark the catch with a triangle cut into the fin. Clearly though, it wasn't without risk.

Satyr hadn't made much of a plan, but fishermen and dockworkers still roamed despite the time, so the front door wasn't going to work. As casually as he could, he sauntered up the side staircase. The second story door was firm, and his stomach dropped as he moved to the third. The handle was locked, but he offered it a firm shoulder, sliding in and nestling it closed, hoping the sound of the wood splintering hadn't alerted anyone.

It was pitch black. The wooden floorboards creaked under his feet, making him cringe. Blind, he fumbled along, finding little except boxes covered in dusty sheets—cargo abandoned for legality or taxation problems and left to rot for years. His heart thundered as he followed the wall around until he found the staircase down. The second floor had sparse, flickering candles. Enough to see that it was neat, stacked wall to wall with wooden crates, some open, some sealed with labels denoting time and ownership. Still, none of the shipments were dated earlier than two weeks ago.

He tried his best to be sneaky when he got to the bottom floor, really, he did. But the windows were large and uncovered by design, the floor groaned in protest against him, and who was going to miss a seven foot, bumbling orc? What he needed was near the side, labeled for Beron. He cracked the top and gagged as the scent of rotting fish puffed into his face. A squawk split the air, sending his heart into a tailspin. A large, colorful bird sat on a perch in the middle of the room. Its head swiveled to the side, one large eye boring into him.

His hands moved in a rush, plucking the handful of fish with split fins. Practiced fingers meant the pearls slipped out of their mouths with ease.

The bird squawked and squawked again, and this time Satyr realized why.

Shuffling steps echoed up the back hallway.

He sealed the box as quietly as he could and retreated toward the second floor—and then tripped through the third. The boards groaned under his weight and as he stole down the open stairs outside, the broken door caught in the wind and slammed back, sending him sprinting as shouts rang from within the building. No pursuit came, but the hair on the back of his neck stood on end until he made it to the relative safety of the inn.

Once inside, he barred both doors and stored the pearls in the secret storeroom behind the pantry. Presley waited on standby to take them to Lamel, so he'd send word in the morning.

It wasn't everything he was owed—Beron likely got caught with the rest—but it would be enough for now. He expected more product next week, from his remaining two harvesters, though whether they would be spooked by Beron's plight he didn't know.

As he finally allowed himself to lay in bed, he thought of Elanie, just across the hall. She'd really pulled through for him today; she'd picked up his slack in the dining room and hummed alongside his singing as they prepared muffins and, of course, more of her famous cinnamon rolls. By evening, her dark-brown eyes were sunken with exhaustion, and he knew she'd pushed herself too hard for his benefit. Coming home to help him each day meant she'd been working two jobs. She couldn't keep it up—even if her presence did make his evenings brighter.

He should do something for her to show his appreciation. And then he should brainstorm what to do when Sybil was unable to help at all. The girl was determined to work with a baby on her back and that was all well and good, but it didn't account for the weeks of rest she'd need no matter what. Satyr wouldn't accept her help, at the very least, but he couldn't expect Elaine to step in the way she did today.

He scrubbed his face. When did his life go from facing a problem head on to hiding in the shadows? From an honest dream of running an inn to being reliant on a job he never wanted in order to survive, in order to help the few people he could?

The smuggling had already doomed Beron. And if somehow they found out about Satyr . . . What would Elaine say when the guard arrived to pick him up? Where would Sybil go? Her newborn? Why did he think he could help anyone?

The night slipped by like grains in a cursed hourglass, reluctant to turn.

"Are you alright?" Elaine asked.

He smiled, and she cocked her head at him, seeing too much. "I didn't sleep well," he said, offering her the packed lunch. She hesitated, and he forced a laugh. "I'm fine, Elaine. Don't be late." He planted a quick kiss on the top of her head and she smiled shyly, face flushing as she looked around at the mostly empty dining area and fled out the door in a grinning fluster.

The other diners trickled in. Breakfast, he didn't have a hard time with—usually the only customers were the ones who stayed the night. Lunch was a little busier, but dinner kept him moving even with Sybil's help. He'd told her he didn't need her to work at least until lunch, and he hadn't seen her leave. He had half a mind to take her breakfast, but thought better of it. She might still be sleeping, and she could use all the rest she could get.

Wrapping two of the muffins—blueberry with a crunchy topping of sugar and a perfectly moist center, he promised himself he'd offer her breakfast *and* lunch when she came down.

Presley arrived just before lunch. Satyr offered him a tankard and went back to the storeroom, careful to keep the door closed behind him. The nondescript box opened with a subtle click. Four pearls. Not much. But enough for now.

He wrapped them and pulled a few hard apples and a loaf of bread to wrap as well, tying the whole of it together with paper and twine.

Presley lifted a brow when Satyr set the package before him. "Sending me with lunch again?"

Satyr grinned. "Who exactly do you think you're talking to?"

"Only the best orc on this side of the Grass Sea."

Satyr chuckled and slapped the man on his shoulder. "Save your flattery for the guards on your way out. And take care of yourself, you hear?"

"Yeah, yeah, I hear. Don't worry so much."

Presley downed the rest of his drink in one go before setting off. Once Satyr was sure the components were on their way to the people who needed them, he was able to breathe a sigh of relief, grateful that some of the tension in his shoulders finally eased. Payment would arrive in six or seven days, and that would set them up with supplies and next month's *rent*. Usually, he wouldn't count his cockatrices before they hatched, but he didn't have a choice but to move forward with using the last of the inn's money for a supply run—they were getting dangerously low on flour.

He did a sweep of the dining room with muscle memory alone. "Everyone doing alright?" he asked, his mind far off as he cleared empty dishes from an occupied table.

The couple looked up from their food, surprised, but not wary of him—they'd visited often enough, though they'd never stayed the night, so he assumed they lived in Arnell. One had short horns curling out of her brown hair, the other was neither feminine nor masculine, with eyes whose irises were split between brown and blue.

"Good!" they said. "It was excellent. We were just saying how Sybil looks like the babe will come any day now."

He grinned, though his worry mounted back up on itself with the reminder. "I tell her the same every day. Doesn't seem to slow her down."

They laughed politely and Satyr carried himself to the next table to clear a few more dishes before heading back into the kitchen. But the room felt smaller, the walls curling around to suffocate him with heat. He stepped out the back, seeking the sanctuary of fresh air and wider space. In Tuskala, the ceilings were taller. He'd spent a year in Arnell before putting his finger on that particular problem.

A rustle had him jerking sideways, taken off guard by the movement in his peripheral.

"Big day?" Ayala asked, a wide smile splitting her furred, deer-like face in two. The jewels on her horns jingled as she moved toward him.

Satyr straightened, trying not to let his exhaustion show. "Hey Ayla."

"Greetings. I saw your friend. She was looking into the windows. I think maybe you should talk to her."

"About what?"

She shrugged. "Anything. Everything. Letting someone know you is a powerful thing."

16

Satyr

BY THE TIME ELAINE made it back from the castle, Satyr had fallen further into his low spirits. She seemed tired, and he was loath to add to her burdens, so he kept his voice light as he entwined their fingers and smoothed his thumb over the back of her hand.

"Would you like to go to the shops with me this evening?"

She grinned, her face lighting up like the dawn, taking his breath away. He couldn't help a chuckle at the sight. The mirth bubbled out of him, and he pressed his forehead to hers for a brief moment, soaking her in, holding melancholy far at bay.

"I'd love to. Just let me get changed," she said, squeezing his hand.

He nodded. "Of course. And I'll let Sybil know we will be back before long."

When Elaine returned, she wore a dark, long-sleeved dress with a cut that complimented her generous figure. She'd braided the shimmering silk into her hair again, letting it hang to one side and allowing his eye catch on the curve of her neck. He blinked at her shy smile, realizing he was staring.

"You're beautiful."

She chuffed, shrugging her shoulders. "I haven't worn this one in a while. Seemed like a good time for it."

Satyr rather thought any moment of any day might have been a good time for it, but instead of speaking, he offered an arm, and she looped it with her own.

The sun had long since begun its descent, sending pinks and oranges skipping on the waves of the sea. . He guided them past the traveler's market and into the city's supply district. Flags waved cheery greetings in the ever-present wind. They needed sugar, more flour, salt, and lemon juice—the kind canned into little glass jars. When the shopkeeper at The Watery Chef told him the total, Satyr pulled out his coin purse, but Elaine stepped between him and the counter.

"You have to admit that price is a bit steep." Her eyebrows pulled together as she looked between him and the shopkeeper.

The man's amiable face soured instantly. "Been a lot going on. Prices go up. That's just the way of things. Besides, you won't find better anywhere else in the city."

Elaine shook her head. "I made an order for the castle *days* ago. Prices haven't changed that drastically. And your flour scoop looks like it hasn't been washed in days. I'm certain we'd have no trouble at all finding better, perhaps at

Argyle's General store?" She looked back to Satyr, her dark eyes imploring him to agree.

"Ah—"

"—You don't work for the castle," the man interrupted.

She turned back to him and grinned, tilting her head in a way that invited him to reconsider.

The shopkeeper's eyes reassessed her, his eyes catching on the Dagadan silk in her hair. He splayed his hands on the counter and leaned forward so far Satyr had to clamp his fists against the urge to punch him. "Fine. Ten silvers."

Elaine wasn't cowed. "Nine."

"Nine," the man bit out. "And you never come back."

Elaine clinked the coins between them before Satyr even had his coin purse in hand.

"Elaine," he rumbled, feeling a bit flustered. "I was gonna pay for that."

"Nonsense." Her eyes sparkled with success as she bagged their goods. "You'll just have to plan on buying dinner over the weekend."

He smiled softly, taking the burden from her as they left. "Was there somewhere specific you had in mind?"

"Ha, anywhere not run by swindlers. Why'd you try to pay? You had to know he was gouging you."

That rankled him a bit, and he sighed, conceding she was right. He'd been noticing that particular shop's price rising a bit every time he visited. Not enough to question. But it was more every time. "I'm . . . not interested in making any trouble."

Her eyes tracked the wagons that rolled by, her tone flippant. "It's not troublesome to expect a fair market price."

The weight on his shoulders grew. "Elaine . . . What if that *was* the price he needed to sell at to make a profit, and I questioned him, and he felt"—satyr shrugged—" . . . intimidated?"

She lifted her chin to bat her eyelashes at him and he couldn't help a grin at the way the movement invited him to admire the graceful cut of her dress and the smooth skin kissed by Arnell's sweet air.

"You're hardly the most intimidating creature in Arnell," she said, her voice a low caress.

He looked at her sideways, raising an eyebrow, trying and failing not to preen under her attention. "You might be one of the few that holds that opinion."

She tsked. "You're kind—and perceptive. Anyone who has spoken to you and heard your voice or your laugh would know, on instinct, that you're a good male."

His stomach squeezed. Was he good? He'd never been truly concerned about the laws of Arnell—this wasn't his home, wasn't his people. His loyalties didn't lie here.

He glanced at Elaine.

At least they didn't use to.

He'd only seen a handful of orcs around the city. There were a few giant kin that lived here, some only slightly larger than he, but infinitely more normalized as they often worked for some noble family or another. Tuskalan orcs were respected, of course, especially as craftsmen—blacksmiths. But their fierce reputation followed him wherever he went, and when he first fled, he encountered many who were nervous. Arnell had lawstones to protect them from the monsters that plagued the Atlas World. Orcs had their fists.

"I'm not saying it's right, Elaine. I'm just saying it makes sense."

She huffed. "It does not *make sense*."

He shrugged again, the parcels lifting along with his shoulders. "It just seems wrong to haggle with someone who might worry I could hurt them if they say no."

"Anyone in this city could hurt them. You don't have to be an orc to be an ass."

The space between them was cool the rest of the way to the inn, but he didn't think her frustration was with him. Sure, his unwillingness to haggle meant a shopkeeper or two might know him as more generous—or an easier mark—but he couldn't put himself in the position of wondering if he'd influenced them in the wrong way. Even if he skimmed pearls for now, the possibility of undercutting local businesses wouldn't do him or the inn any good long term.

That she believed him to be so *good* meant her arguments were unfounded—and made his gut churn. *She* was good. She was diligent in her work with the castle, and generous with her time and her help. She offered politely to help with the cooking, but swept in without comment when he fell behind in the dining room, and he'd shooed her away from scouring dishes on more than one occasion. She worried over Sybil. Worried over him. Defended him.

She was good.

He smiled and shook his head as they came in the door to find Sybil toting the large tray around, and Elaine instantly took it from the girl and headed back to the kitchen. Sybil gave him a relieved grin in greeting and returned to the counter for a towel. As usual, only a couple tables were occupied now, with patrons chatting and nursing half-empty drinks

He followed Elaine into the kitchen, and she opened the pantry for him without a word, but she stood in the doorway watching as he put their bounty away, keeping everything on shelves she could reach.

"I'm sorry," she said.

He paused, caught off guard. "For what?"

She sighed, slouching against the door frame. "For . . . getting in the middle of things . . . For you having to deal with it at all . . ." She watched him with mournful eyes. "For not being more understanding."

Gravity itself had him moving closer, or perhaps some other force he'd yet to name, but held a much stronger sway. One moment, he stood with a gritty, leaking bag of sugar. The next he'd curled an arm around her waist and pressed his head to hers. "I don't know what the right answer is, Elaine. I only know how I've managed this long. I don't think you should apologize. I just . . ." He pressed a kiss into her hair. "No matter what, I'm grateful for you. For seeing the best of me, and reminding me it's there."

She still looked sad, so he pressed a soft kiss to her lips too.

She responded in kind, curling her fingers in his hair, the sweet sting a demand he was happy to meet. With half a thought, he pulled her past the threshold and clicked the door closed, relishing her sharp intake of breath as he pressed his hands on either side of her. She grinned, face flushing, eyes already glassy with the same heady feelings pumping through his veins.

"May I kiss you again, Elaine?" he asked, as her eyes flickered to his lips.

"You just were, why ask now?"

"You're right, let me be more clear." He leaned forward until his mouth rested on the curve of her ear. "May I kiss you with intent to impassion? May I kiss you until you're trembling with need? May I lift you with an arm, trap you against this wall, and drive away every sense of awareness but that of our mingling breath?"

She'd gone completely still.

He brushed a tusk up her neck, breathing in her scent of warm, sugary vanilla.

"I'm not sure you can lift me."

He tried not to snort. "May I prove you wrong?"

He held breath while she hesitated.

"You can try."

He had her up in an instant, one arm scooped underneath. "Oh!"

He grinned at the redness in her cheeks. She wrapped her legs around him, but there was no need. He kept her aloft with one splayed hand, but leveraged his body to pin her to the door with his waist. She surprised him by curling her hips, seeking. He paused, and she grinned. The challenge had him adjusting so she could feel how interested he was in her teasing.

"Satyr!" she squealed as he easily maneuvered her, but she stilled abruptly, eyes wide. "Is that—?"

His voice rumbled through his chest. "It seems you have quite the effect on me, Elaine."

"Well *you* have quite the—well. You're quite gifted, sir."

He squeezed her hips, relishing the way her body spilled through his fingers.

The soft little moan she gave in return had him even harder. With one hand, he held her. The other he twisted into the back of her hair and pulled just firm enough for her to yield her mouth. He teased his tongue over her lips, the way she'd done before and she groaned in protest as he instead kissed his way over her jaw, down her neck, and took his time trailing back up to her ear, her skin impossibly soft on his lips, angling so the tips of his tusks only barely grazed her as he went.

All the while, she sought friction against him. Already, the mere brush of her over their clothing had a blistering, greedy heat pooling low in his gut. There was a good chance he'd be finished from this alone. It had been too long since he'd had a woman, and to have *this* woman? How had a single spice brought him the single most perfect creature in all of existence?

"Do you know how stunning you are, Elaine?"

She scoffed. Actually scoffed, and he stopped, pinning her harder so she had to stop as well.

"What was that?" he asked, as if he'd misheard the answer. "You *are* aware of how ravishing you are?"

She grinned, fighting uselessly to move her body against his strength. "I never said that."

He squeezed tighter, angling his waist, giving her the friction her body continued to seek. She groaned, dropping her head back onto the door and as she went pliant, he swung her to the freezer nearby, tucking her dress up to settle his body even closer against her.

She leaned back on her elbows, and he followed her down, finally kissing her lips. The sensation was always strange, but delicious. He all but trembled at the feeling of her tongue sweeping over his lips, wanting more. When he opened, she kissed him with renewed fervor, lifting and hooking both hands over the back of his neck. He couldn't help the low groan that escaped him as she drew them closer with her legs, clinging to every bit of touch.

"We probably," she said between kisses, "shouldn't—do this—in—the pantry."

"Probably," he rumbled, squeezing an arm between them. She gasped as his knuckles grazed over the wetness that formed on her underclothes.

"Elaine," he rumbled, all but defeated already.

"Don't stop," she said.

"Oh shii—!" Sybil exclaimed, sweeping out the door as fast as she'd entered.

He and Elaine righted themselves in a scramble, but Sybil was gone. Elaine's face had flamed impossibly pinker. It only made her swollen lips look more delicious.

17

Elaine

Sybil was in the dining room, wiping down the last of the tables. She didn't give them the chance to explain. "Talilah was looking for you," she called.

"What did you tell her?" Satyr said, his voice too careful.

Elaine peered at him. Was it the woman she'd seen?

"That you were busy." Sybil grinned, lifting her eyebrows, then burst out laughing. "Oh the look on your faces. Why are you so embarrassed? How do you think I got like this?" She gestured to her rounded belly. Her laugh echoed through the empty inn, contagious enough that Elaine smiled, though she wondered about the mystery woman, and why she would seek Satyr out as the inn closed its doors for the day.

The next morning, she woke in her own bed.

She'd been too embarrassed to suggest they renew their interests the night before, and her stomach quaked with an interesting mix of anticipation and nerves as she walked down the stairs. To her disappointment, Satyr wasn't in the dining room. Every morning since she'd begun to stay here, he'd greeted her at the door with food to take. The kitchen was empty too, and suddenly she couldn't help but feel a bit presumptuous. After all, she was capable of making her own lunch.

The walk to the castle was foggy, and as she approached, an odd number of guards stood, peppered around the city, growing denser the nearer she got.

"Good morning!" she sang as she entered the kitchen. Airam had been arriving before her more and more often. He'd already begun the breakfast prep, and Roman stood by, washing dishes as they were dirtied. She hung her cloak and stepped next to him to wash her hands. "Are we in a hurry today?"

Airam turned. "His Majesty sent orders this morning that we are to begin preparing rations and travel food. Two weeks worth for over a dozen men. Hopefully he's sourcing from the city too, because it will take us days. We figured we better get a head start."

The news had Elaine in high gear. Dishes rattled, pans scraped, breakfast was finished, and she helped Roman carry the extra smokers outside. Most of the staff prepped the meat, while Elaine cataloged what they could use from the pantry. Lunch was a stuffed ham—a welcome break from the usual seafood fare—with creamy sliced potatoes and some of the last of the garden's salad greens. Otherwise, she'd have to make a rush order for the market for whatever was on hand already—there was no time to be picky. After confirming the traveling party would include a cook, she made the list, double checked the smokers, and met the delivery crew outside to hand over the market order.

As the wagon rolled away, a vaguely familiar face wandered into the castle courtyard.

The man was tall, with rich golden skin and thin, rectangular glasses perched low on his nose. The badge on his jacket designated him a member of Arnell's estate management. "Miss Galliade!" He waved, his long steps invigorated with purpose as their eyes met. "Our notes didn't say where you planned to live in the interim, but I was hoping to find you here."

"It's Elaine, if you don't mind. Is there something wrong with the house?"

"Something wrong? Why not at all! It's sold. And for ten percent more than the asking price!"

"It's sold?" She waited to feel sorrow, but . . . nothing. She'd already mourned its empty rooms a hundred times over.

The man puffed up. "In this market, I'm not surprised to see it go so quickly. Now, all that's left is for you to sign. Then the money is yours. Are you moving in with a partner?"

The question took her off guard. "No, actually."

"Leaving Arnell then? Well, there's nothing like country living, I've got a few houses available closer to the Corsarian border. There's been an influx of homes put up for sale in that area, but more homes means lower prices and a better deal for you. Do let me know if I can help you find something."

Elaine nodded numbly. "Shall I sign the papers here, then?"

"Unless you'd like to meet the buyers?"

"No." That wouldn't change anything.

He nodded. "Then yes! Yes. Here—" he handed her a clipboard and quill.

She signed before she had time to think about it. It was just a house. She'd lost her home long ago.

The man's eyes lit with excitement. "I'll see to it that the payment is made in your name. Do let me know if you need help again. Ah—Also, now that the showings are done, we will have to arrange pickup for the furniture."

"I don't want it. Sell it."

"All of it?"

She nodded. Panic speared through her as his brow furrowed and he scribbled something down. "Not the plants though! I want them. Would you mind noting that they need to be brought to the Aspen Inn, it's by the traveler's market. And you can take the delivery charge out of the sale price."

He began nodding as he continued to write. "If you're sure, I think that's all we need."

Elaine nodded again and walked away in a haze. That was that. The house was gone. The three bedrooms. The empty living room. The kitchen. She was unsure where she was going until she hit the familiar room. The owner of the trinket store peered at her from the doorway, but said nothing. Elaine stopped outside the inn. Now she had no reason to stay. There was no changing her mind. No going back on the papers she'd signed. The house she'd lived in for the last decade belonged to someone else now. Someone who would fill it with laugher. With children.

At that moment, Satyr opened the door. His brows pinched in concern. "Elaine? You're early . . . What is it?"

"Nothing," she said. He looked as if he were about to argue, and her voice broke as she went on, "I'm thirty-four years old and I have nothing."

He stepped forward and enveloped her in his arms. The cracks in her heart burst wide open, and she clung to his chest, sobbing. Abruptly, she felt herself lifted, and turned her face into his body to hide as he took her through the dining room and up the stairs.

He pushed through the door to her room and laid her on the bed before he said a single word. She cried as he draped the blanket over her and smoothed down her hair. "You have a job many would die for and the talent to have earned it. You have a sharp wit and a smile that could make an angry manticore stop and ask for your favor. You have a heart of gold, and the love others have for you will outlive many fae. You have your experience, your love, and endless patience for a clumsy, food-loving orc."

She huffed a laugh through tears as he moved to the other side of the bed and lay next to her, gently tucking her body into his. The tears came quietly, and he let the silence, and his warmth, say enough. Long after the setting sun peeked through the window she jerked up. "I have to go back. We are prepping rations at the castle. I shouldn't miss dinner."

"Stay." Her heart leapt in her throat at the word. *Stay?* His chest rumbled against her. "Just for tonight," he clarified softly. "Stay. I'll send word to the kitchens that you're out."

Elaine let the idea settle. The others would handle dinner fine. The smokers would have to run until tomorrow whether she was there or not. Plus, they'd only ask her questions she didn't want to answer if they saw her puffy eyes and a radish red nose. She let herself lay back again.

How often had Dara missed the first half of the day? And of course, Airam took time off now and then to be with his husband. No matter if she returned or not, they'd ask questions. But she likely wouldn't be useful either way.

She scooted closer to Satyr, pressing herself into his warmth. "I'm sorry."

He lifted her chin with a finger, forcing her to meet his dark eyes. "Don't," he said seriously.

"I've interrupted your day. I've taken you from your own kitchen."

"This is where I'm needed most." He kissed her hair, then leaned his forehead into hers.

"Even though I'm an unbearable burden?" Her tone was light, with worry folded inside. Already she'd leaned on him more than she should.

He smiled, brushing hair over her ear. "I'm pretty strong."

She laughed, choking on tears. How was it possible to feel such mix of emotions all at once? "I just . . . things are hard, lately."

"Do you want to talk about it?"

Did she? Yes. Would she? No. Not now. Not when she already struggled to breathe with the weight of change bearing down.

He continued, as if she hadn't let the question go unanswered. "You know, when I left Tuskala, I left everything."

She stilled, her head curled into his chest as his hand traced patterns over her shoulder. The sunlight covered his arm with a latticework pattern of shade, illuminating his arms in uneven patches. Where the light touched, he was like spring, and where shaded, his skin was a deep, rich green, unlike anything she'd ever seen. "My family cast me off. They likely pretend my brother and I never existed. Traveling through the Grass Sea was fine, for the most part. I was alone, but capable enough to handle the creatures that wanted to eat me. Once I made it to the three kingdoms, things got harder. Not more dangerous but—" He paused, and she hardly dared to breathe lest it stop him from going on. "Many were suspicious of the shirtless orc carrying so much anger alongside the greatsword in his hand. Rightly so, I suppose. I was as formidable as anything else outside the lawstone's protection.

"But . . . it was lonely. I stayed nowhere for long, looking for work to trade for a full belly. I gathered ingredients. Monster hides. Eliminated pests and chased off predators. I was useful, and some appreciated my ability to do what they could not. I may have been more welcome in Umbri, where giant-kin are more common, where the stocky and durable are preferred. But I wanted to be in Arnell. Something about the color. The smell. The ocean is warmer here, so the air is too, by a little. And the people are happy. It's not perfect. And by orc standards this place is as soft and vulnerable as it gets. But here, there are artists and craftsmen. Chefs and cheery innkeepers with round bellies."

Elain laughed softly at his grin.

"The traveler's market was the first time I saw Tuskalan wares since I'd left home. And though I can never go back, I wanted to be near it, somehow. I wanted a place, like this one, that was mine, a home."

Elaine's eyes welled up again at the word.

"But I had nothing." He cupped a hand over the side of her cheek and brought her eyes to his. "I know what it's like to start over, Elaine. I won't say I've felt what you're feeling. But the ache in me, sees you. I'm here. I'm not going anywhere. You will always have a place to lay your head, even if it's not forever. Someone dear to me once took a chance on a heartbroken orc with more loneliness than good sense. And it made me who I am today."

Who was she, today? No one she recognized. Her voice was a broken whisper. "I just thought my life would be different."

He kissed her head again. "This one can still be good."

She squeezed her eyes shut, curling her entire being around the words as the tears slid sideways to soak into his shirt.

After a while, she stilled, her eyes growing droopy as exhaustion swept in. "I'm going to go down and check on Sybil," he whispered. "Don't leave this bed. I'll bring you something to eat. And hot chocolate?"

She huffed a tired laugh. From random market stranger to closest friend. "Yes, please."

He lit the fire before he left.

18

Satyr

Sybil sat, thankfully, behind the dark wood counter, chatting with the same half-dwarf who'd visited often lately. When she looked over the male's shoulder, Satyr gave her a tight-lipped smile, passing them by to get the kitchen in order for dinner—fish, again, of course. What he wouldn't give for red meat. Still, he let the work ground him, stoking the fires, preparing the knives, parsing through the seasonings. All things he could do blindfolded at this point. Cleaning and fileting was messy, but didn't take long, and was more than worth it to keep the flavor truly fresh. The counter thunked as his kitchen cleaver made quick work of the heads, and a well-loved filet knife managed the rest. The reward came as he tossed them in the lemon oil to sizzle, and the scent rose to meet him. A low rumble in his gut reminded him he missed lunch.

In the moment between deciding he should eat and actually making a plate, the back door of the kitchen swung open, but the sound of footsteps didn't follow.

"I told you to use the front," he growled as he turned around.

"You don't pay any attention to me if I use the front." The dragonblood leaned against the wall, her horns and purple skin muted in the dim light. Her body was lithe, but Satyr knew she was more formidable than many would realize based on looks alone. She studied him with eyes as sharp as knives. "Why have you been so hard to get hold of, orc?"

He tried to keep the exhaustion out of his voice as he tossed the trimmings. "I do more than peddle baubles to you, Talilah. What have you learned?"

She studied her sharpened nails. "They're keeping him in the jailhouse."

Satyr breathed a sigh of relief. There may be hope for the man yet. It presented a unique opportunity. If they hadn't yet moved him to the castle dungeons, Satyr may be able to bribe the guard to free him. The fee would be high. High enough he may not make 'rent.' But no matter the cost, Satyr would pay it, if only so he could sleep at night without the eyes and sorrow of that angry child weighing on him.

"I need an advance on the next delivery," Satyr said, unsurprised when she helped herself to a fork and popped a raw morsel of fish in her mouth.

She chewed thoughtfully before answering. "I thought you might say that. But they're not gonna let him out."

"Why?"

She shrugged, spearing another raw slice. "Because the princess was kidnapped, Umbri's champion was never hanged, and the crown needs a win. They'll kill him just to claim a petty victory."

"I met his son," Satyr said , the room shrinking in on him, condensing the air, pressing him down until he may as well have been underwater for all he could breathe.

She nodded, her voice indifferent as she studied the slices that remained. "A mistake."

Satyr sucked in a breath as he fell onto a dusty stool and wiped his head with an edge of his apron. "I never wanted this."

"You chose the job. *He* chose the job."

"His kid didn't. I think there's a sister too."

Her voice was stone. "Some people grow up without parents."

Helplessness flared hot in his blood, the worry spiking into irritation. "You think I don't know that, Talilah? As it stands, they won't just lose their father they'll lose their citizen status too. The crown has probably already frozen it as it is. So, what? Beron dies. Then no healers if they get sick. Lower priority for employment and higher likelihood of oily fae landlords that'll raise the "rent" every four months just to squeeze blood from stone." He turned his back to scoop a mess of flour from the counter into his hand, but his frustration only sent it into a cloud of white that mocked him on its way to settle on the floor.

Talilah took a few steps closer, but the steel in her voice never wavered. "They will suffer. But not because of you. Because the crown squeezes the life out of anything with value. Because their father was a criminal that was stupid enough to get caught."

"Is," he corrected fiercely as he turned on her. "He is a criminal. And so am I. And so are you. And it could be any of us that ends up there. Tomorrow. Next week." Satyr was tired of feeling helpless, tired of being stuck in the same cycle that meant he could either keep smuggling—or stop eating. Stop *cooking*. Stop being a refuge for those that felt about as welcome in Arnell as he. Skimming pearls wasn't supposed to last long. He never meant to feel responsible for more lives than his own, but the answer seemed so simple once he said it aloud, and resolve silenced his own reservations as he spoke.

"We're breaking him out."

It wasn't nearly as dark as he'd like it to be for this kind of work. As spring lengthened, so did their days and despite the dinner hour, the city was busy, still winding down as the sun touched the horizon. With Elaine tucked in bed, and Sybil managing the dinner he'd left warm on the counter, he took to the main road. He wore a hood and pulled a loaded cart behind him. With his size, many would assume he were any of the giant-kin, a fact he hoped to lean into to avoid suspicion. Eyes forward, he let the chattering crowd part around him, determined to *do* something. He needed to see the jailhouse with his own eyes.

It appeared with no fanfare. Squat and relatively drab compared to the buildings around it, the jailhouse was small for a city the size of Arnell, mostly used for drunks or as a processing point. Only the castle dungeons held criminals long term. A single guard sat outside. There'd be another inside, or more, depending on how occupied it was. Either way, if reinforcements were called, it wouldn't take long for them to arrive. Anyone with eyes could see that guard patrol was heavier than usual on the main road leading to the castle. Satyr turned right, avoiding a group of them on his way back to Talilah.

Her cape and deep cowl rippled in the shelter of a thin alley. "How many?"

"One outside." If they had more time, he'd be able to get more information, make a better plan.

Her mouth twitched up. "Want me to kill him?"

"*Disarm* him," he ordered. "But we do nothing until tomorrow."

She scoffed, refusing to look at him.

He wasn't going to let her draw more attention to them than necessary, but he kept his voice even, letting his frustration bleed from his tightened hands and away into the cart handles. "Masters not letting you off the leash often enough?"

She had a blade to his throat in an instant. "Watch it, orc."

He pressed into her, forcing her to give ground or slit his throat. She took measured steps back, her eyes hard, but didn't lower the blade.

His voice was low. "Your recklessness won't help anyone."

She snarled and ripped away. "They're impatient! They want more. And I can't do it without the pearls. The sooner we get back on track the less they'll breath down my neck."

He grabbed the cart and began walking, fighting the dips of the cobblestone road. "Have you considered finding other employment?" He tossed the words over his shoulder as if he were asking if she'd prefer peach jam over narlberry jelly.

Talilah was a rare magic user, a dragonblood of some origin or another. He wasn't well versed in her abilities beyond a need for components, though her blood alone could be used in ritual magic. Satyr wouldn't be surprised if she sprouted wings and flew one day, but he'd never asked, and why she stayed under the thumb of her keepers, he didn't know.

She didn't move to follow as he put distance between them. "We meet tomorrow," she called before letting herself fade into the busy thoroughfare.

"Tomorrow." He murmured over a heaved breath.

Surely he was getting too old for jailbreaks and threats. One day, he would be free. He'd get the inn profitable. Somehow. Maybe they could host a craftsperson or two. Start selling books or soaps or anything else that might draw interest. Then, he could pass this side of the business on to someone with more ambition. And he'd spend the rest of his days cooking good food.

19

Elaine

ELAINE COULDN'T MAKE IT out of bed the next morning.

Try as she might, the weight on her chest was too heavy. Satyr came to check on her in the morning, her usually wrapped breakfast in hand. "I'll send a messenger to the castle to let them know you're sick. I think it's a good day to rest."

"Don't go out of your way." She'd inconvenienced him enough as it is.

"It's not out of my way. It's a note and a coin. And since you're here, I can make you something special for breakfast."

No part of her was hungry. "You don't have to trouble yourself."

He leaned over and pressed his lips to her forehead. "I like being troubled by you. I'll be back."

She woke again, surrounded by a funeral's silence. The biscuits and pork gravy he'd left while she'd slept had gone cold and stiff.

She blinked, and suddenly the sun was low, barely peeking over the ocean to touch on Arnell. He sat on her bed, holding a clay cup, brows pinched in concern as he studied her. "A ghrá. Would you mind drinking some of this for me?"

She sat up and took the cup, hot chocolate. "A ghrá?"

He smiled softly. "A term of endearment in Tuskala, though I don't know the word in common. I can stick with Elaine, if you prefer"

She shook her head and took a small sip. "I don't mind." The quiet was too heavy, so she spoke again. "How were things today?" She could feel the warmth radiating through the blanket and into her legs.

"The inn? Same as ever." After a moment he went on, "Think you'll be up to eating dinner?"

She nodded, if only to ease the worried gleam in his eye.

"In here?" he asked.

She sat up a little further and eased her legs to the floor." I can go down to the kitchen with you."

"Okay, but you're not allowed to help," he said, reading her like a book.

"You need all the help you can get and I—" She paused. Her father was gone. The house was gone. Her old life was gone, for better or worse, but there were some things that never changed. "I need to cook."

He considered the words, then dipped his head slowly.

They'd propped the back door open, but still sweat streaked down the side of her face. Two tablespoons of oil. A small onion, chopped. Two cloves of garlic, minced of course. Crushed tomatoes. A couple fish worth of filets. Rolls in the stone oven. Boiling rutabaga on the stove, almost ready to be mashed. Elaine let herself get lost to the scents and measurements. As the night wore on, the dining room became packed tight with bodies, fuller than she'd ever seen it. Groups from one table leaned over to chatter with another. Some stood against the wall, nursing steins and eyeing the paper lanterns on the ceiling. Satyr handled each with a graceful smile, even those that were . . . surprised to be served by an orc. Still, others joked loudly with him, and Satyr's booming laugh raised the uneasy spirits of the whole room.

"We've got more coming in," he said, sweeping through the kitchen door. Elaine managed the stove while Sybil washed dishes as fast as she could.

"Did you announce a sale?" Elaine asked, incredulous. "Where is everyone coming from?"

"The king announced a festival this morning! Apparently, everyone from the outer cities started arriving late this afternoon!"

"A festival, for what?"

Satyr filled a row of dripping steins. "For the glory of Arnell!" His eyes twinkled. "We may run out of ale altogether." The contagious glee had her smiling, and their eyes caught. In one swift motion he'd hooked an arm around her waist and brought her close, clutching her other hand to his chest as he swayed them in a circle. "It's good to see your smile again, a ghrá."

She huffed a laugh. "You're happy."

He leaned his forehead to hers. "I am."

They swayed a moment longer, until the telltale sound of a clattering mug pulled them apart.

"Does anyone have a cloth?" someone called from the dining room.

He stopped. "I could never have managed this night without you." He kissed her forehead before spiriting through the door, cloth in one hand and three dripping steins in the other."

Soon, Thorin started playing. The melody was familiar, and as soon as he started singing, Elaine's heart caved back in on itself. The words seemed sadder than before, though they were the same as they'd always been.

The water she sees me
The waves bid me come
Come and then be free
Her beckoning hum
Were I to go
I'd ne'er return
The water its song bid me stay
Stay and don't suffer
For the absence of land
Naught but heartache lay that way.

Elaine stirred the pot through frustrated tears.

There was nothing to stop her from leaving now. She needed to leave. Needed to put this city behind her. She'd be betraying herself if she stayed.

"Elaine." Elaine jumped. Sybil gently took the serving spoon from her hand. An acrid scent let her know she'd burned the garlic. The whole thing would have to be remade. A different, more spirited song played in the dining room.

"I'm so sorry," Elaine said, hands too slow to fix the mess.

"It happens to everyone. You okay?" Sybil knocked the pan over the waste basket and Elaine followed as she set it in the sink. The heat made it steam as she waved Elaine away and began to scrub it.

"I can't get have children." The words were a whisper.

Sybil's hands paused, but continued scouring after a moment. "You've been trying?"

Elaine swallowed. Swallowed again. "I tried. For years. For a decade. We lost every one." The words could barely squeeze past the lump in her throat. "Things got bad with my partner. We couldn't get past it. And then it was just me. The house. It was empty. But I couldn't leave because I thought—" she cut off, because the truth was absurd, only she hadn't realized it while she lived it.

"You thought you deserved it," Sybil said softly.

Elaine cracked a bit more. Tears flowing quietly down her cheeks.

The woman smiled at her softly. "I feel the same way sometimes. About all of this." She waved her hand over her rounded belly.

That made Elaine bite back a sob, and Sybil came over to embrace her.

"I'm sorry." Elaine shook her head. "I shouldn't be dumping all of this on you. Not when you're already carrying so much."

"Many hands make for a lighter load," the woman rumbled, in what was obviously her best impression of Satyr.

The unexpected humor made Elaine laugh, and that made her tears begin in earnest.

The orc in question walked in, but Sybil didn't let go of Elaine. She shooed him with a hand. "Girl stuff."

He nodded, snatched the last wicker basket full of rolls off the counter, and veered out the door again.

"This isn't the life I expected either," Sybil murmured, her head nestled against Elaine's shoulder. "But it's still good."

Still good.

The words slowly seeped into the cracks in her heart. After a long moment, they stepped back to their own tasks, and Sybil's voice was hesitant. "Was there nothing the healers could do for you? Any magic?"

Elaine nodded as she wiped her eyes. Having grown up in Corsair, Sybil wouldn't fully understand the magic of the Fae. "We tried. Magic will only bring something back to what it was. It doesn't heal someone who is born unable to see, or give someone what they were born without. The healer I spoke to thought it was beautiful that the magic would always view me as whole." Elaine's eyes misted at the memory. The words had been an insult, at the time. "There are non-magical doctors as well, of course. But their remedies made little difference for me."

"I imagine it must be hard for many people, that it heals injury but little else."

That was true. Some were born with illnesses they'd have for a lifetime. Others, without sight or hearing, with no reason and no way out. Surgeons could do their work without fear though, if there were a skilled healer on hand, and that was enough for many.

The dining room bell chimed, and Sybil passed Elaine the clean pan. "I'm always here if you need to talk."

Elaine pressed her lips into a smile, already embarrassed for letting the truth spill from her so unexpectedly. She and Sybil weren't exactly close. Still, the young woman seemed to understand better than many.

Satyr decided to keep the dining room open an hour later but sent her and Sybil away. Elaine gave little argument. The dining room was only half full now. She laid in her bed and stared at the ceiling, waiting for sleep to take her. Her body ached. Gods, her feet felt like swollen sausages. Sure, she stood all day at the castle, but the haste of managing the crowd in the inn was different than overseeing a few cooks and directing servants to carry food in a specific order. Satyr may not have survived this night without an extra set of hands—had hardly survived *with* her help. But he'd done beautifully all the same. Every person got a warm smile and his genuine interest. Each meal hit the table hot. It was a wonder they weren't this full all the time. Perhaps it had something to do with the place being out of the way, or perhaps it could only draw in those who would have no issues being served by an orc who had modeled the building after his home. Meeting him and seeing the beauty of this place would sweep those concerns away.

The fireplace wasn't lit. She considered lighting it. The fog brought a damp chill to the air, but she let the thought go. It wasn't that she wasn't capable. It was just so . . . intimate. A warm fire in the hearth for a meal for two, for a cozy evening on the couch reading or playing table games. In her old life, the routine had been so ingrained that she hadn't noticed it anymore. Now, it was as if she could see *him* kneeling by the bricks, flint and steel in hand, grinning in a way she hadn't seen for much longer than he'd been gone from her life.

There'd been no one for her since. For two years she'd taken life one day at a time. Go to work, avoid going home as long as possible, return to sleep and do it all over again. That was her new routine.

But this? This had been fun. They'd had to send for more food in the middle of dinner and nearly ran out of ale as well. Of course, most were there because a last-minute festival meant there was little availability elsewhere, but Satyr had navigated the nervous energy with ease. It wouldn't surprise her if the inn found itself with a few more regulars. Though, if it got busy daily, they'd no longer be able to make things work without extra hands. Then they'd really have to consider hiring a washperson, or another barkeep.

Elaine shook her head, chastising herself for the seed of ambition that had planted itself in her. Satyr had it running how he saw fit. It was his inn.

20

Satyr

Satyr nearly didn't notice the thief. He must have slipped in during the rush, seeing as he was small enough to be obscured by larger bodies. Another cup clattered to the ground, and there was an exclamation, but this time he noticed the small form flicking around, lithe, as he swiped payment from a table while many were distracted with the mess.

Satyr met him in the middle of the room. "I don't believe that belongs to you."

He'd known some would slip out without paying, and on this night the boy may have gotten away with it, were luck on his side.

"Well I do believe you stink like lizard shit," the boy said as he looked up.

Satyr blinked. Before he had time to register that it was Beron's son, the boy's face contorted and he took off, knocking an empty chair over in an effort to slow pursuit.

None came.

Customers watched Satyr curiously, their eyes flickering from him to the door that hung open. He moved to it and eased it closed, trying to keep himself grounded. The boy seemed surprised to find him, so he hadn't come here on purpose. He'd fled, but knew Satyr recognized him.

Why would he be stealing? Worry twisted in his gut. He'd have to make another visit, but not until they freed Beron. No use giving him false hope in telling him their plan before they'd seen it through.

The night wore on, and he steeled his nerves as the last of the patrons shuffled out or found rooms. At the stroke of midnight Talilah appeared in the kitchen just as Satyr tucked a note under a pan, just in case they didn't make it back. He was confident in their plan, and he'd made the necessary preparations, but it seemed better to be ready for the worst. With luck, they'd be back in time for him to get a few hours of sleep.

He followed Talilah down the dark, foggy streets. They'd both dressed in neutral, long sleeve tunics, trousers, and thin garden gloves. His feet ached with every step. It had been a busy day, and with any luck, it would be the same tomorrow. Some of the crowd seemed to enjoy the Tuskalan spin to much of his food. Perhaps he should lean into it more, rather than relying on the sea-based dishes popular in Arnell. Meat from the north had always been too expensive to make financial sense, but if they drew in a larger crowd, it might be worth considering. Of course, if he managed to bring in a crowd more often, he'd have to hire more help, which meant he'd need to be able to reliably pay them.

Talilah gave him a sharp look as he sighed. She was right. He needed to keep his head straight if they were going to do this. Around the corner from the jailhouse, they watched the single guard stationed out front. Right on time, a scream ripped through the night. The woman on guard jolted upright and then ran toward the sound.

As soon as she'd gone, Satyr donned a sheep festival mask and watched as Talilah hid her face with an expertly sculpted dragon head with openings for her own horns. It seemed the crafters were working double time to prepare for the festivities, and Talilah has taken advantage, though he hadn't missed her smirk when she'd made him the sheep.

Once her disguise was secure, she nodded. A few quick steps later he put the weight of his body into the jailhouse door, splintering it off its hinges. Two guards flew up at the commotion, but Satyr was already swinging, throwing his entire weight behind the fist he threw at the man's jaw. A distant pain flickered through him as his knuckles split on the second swing. The guard staggered backward, dazed and collapsed onto the ground. Satyr stretched his fingers against the ache as he turned toward the man Talilah had put down, checking for the rise and fall of his chest.

"He's fine," she said testily.

"Thank you."

The inside of the building mirrored the outside: all drab stone and sharp corners. Satyr swiped a ring of keys from the wall. A few of the prisoners stood behind sections of dark iron bars, watching with keen eyes.

"Are you letting us out?"

"No." Satyr walked down the single row, looking for Beron.

"Well why the fuck not? Got the keys in your hand."

"Why are you in here?"

The man opted not to answer. There was little chance Satyr would release a criminal whose crime he didn't know. Smuggling was one thing. Even thieving. But some crimes didn't deserve mercy.

"My family will starve without me," the man continued. "My wife can't work."

"Talilah, is there a list in there?"

"You want to free them?"

A fae woman behind the bars watched intently.

"A few." It would help obscure their motive if nothing else. Satyr studied the man, as Talilah rifled around..

"Cell number six," she read aloud. "Yorgen Frenis. Domestic violence."

The man cursed as Satyr passed him by. Talilah continued, reading each name and suspected crime, and Satyr unlocked the doors of those willing. Some preferred to chance staying.

"Be a shame if the guards got a good description of you two: a monstrously tall male, let me guess, giant kin? And a lusty female with horns."

Talilah stalked toward his cell, and Satyr turned his back to unlock Beron's door. The man sat on the cot, elbows resting on his knees, head bowed.

"You came for me." His voice was gravely, like the rumble of a wagon wheel.

"I did, but we need to go."

Beron's shadowed eyes rose to meet his. "You know I won't be able to stay in Arnell."

Satyr stepped to the side, letting the gate whine open on long suffering hinges. "No. You won't. But we can talk once we're out of here."

The man sighed, shaking his head. "I can't bring my family into this."

"They may be better off escaping with you."

"No. Running isn't a life for a kid. I'll probably end up all the way in the Mire islands."

They were running out of time. "Then find a way to carve a new life, Beron. And when you send word, I will get them to you."

"Just send them my love, will you? Tell them . . . tell them I'm sorry."

Satyr nodded, and Beron stood, moving to the opening.

A heavy thud sounded behind them and Talilah turned away from the now unconscious man in the cell. "Ready when you are, boss."

Satyr nodded, his mask filling with hot air as he spoke. "Take half left, I'll take the other half right. Keep to the shadow—"

Her head tipped back, and he couldn't see it, but he could *feel* her eyes roll. "I know what I'm doing."

"Can I be in your group?" a nervous-looking man piped in, his face split in half with a thin mustache.

Satyr hardly gave him a glance. "No." There was no good reason for Satyr to refuse, other than the fact that the dubious look he gave Talilah irritated him. Satyr lifted his voice to address everyone. "If either group gets spotted, *do not run*. Or you'll damn the lot of us." He turned to Tahlilah. "I'll meet you at the back."

She nodded before leading her group out the door. Immediately, one of the prisoners took off at a sprint. Damn. They'd mapped the guard rounds as well as they could, and had a window of safety, but not in that direction. He gestured the others forward, and as they paced through narrow streets and alleyways, shouts rang in that direction.

"Let's move." Satyr broke into a jog, his chest heaving, his left knee twinging alongside his angry feet. They rounded a corner, and came face to face with a pair of guards.

Satyr swayed, the action not completely feigned. "Good evening, sirs! Sir—and Madam!" he said, slurring the words together. His voice was muffled through the sheep mask. Their only hope was that the guards had yet to be alerted to the escape.

"State your business." The first guard spoke while the second eyed his four companions warily.

"My business?" Satyr hooked his arms around the two nearest him. One grunted under his weight. "I'm getting maaarrrrried!"

One of the escapees caught on. "We were just taking him home, miss. His wedded will be pissed if he doesn't get some sleep at some point before the morning."

The guards assessed them. "What's got you on the street? And what's with the mask?"

The longer they stayed here the more likely it became that alarm bells would start ringing from the jailhouse.

"Ah," the prisoner to the other side laughed, "he said he wanted to, 'wool the world.'"

A snort echoed from another in the group.

The first guard laughed. "Then you should see to it," they said, tossing their head in a gesture for Satyr and company to pass. "Just ensure he isn't disturbing the peace much longer.

"Will do, thanks."

Satyr let the group carry him, his steps clumsy, until they made it to the residential district.

"Unless you want out of the city, this is where we split. Walk normally. If any of you get caught, keep your lips sealed. I don't forget names." His voice rumbled low. "Anyone who wants out of the city, stay with me."

Two left, a couple of thin kids who'd likely worked the streets a while. Beron and another man stayed, their shoulders set in acceptance.

He took the mask off, relishing the taste of fresh air, and didn't miss the second man's surprise at seeing an orc beneath the disguise. "Very well. Follow me."

Satyr took them to the inn. All was dark in the kitchen, but he lit the stove and set a pot out for tea. They'd made a basket of muffins for the morning, so Satyr offered each man one. Only Beron accepted.

The other man seemed bewildered. "Nice place you have here."

"Thank you," Satyr said, the words genuine.

"What will you tell my family?" Beron interrupted, his voice gravelly.

Satyr sighed. "The truth, most likely." He told the man how his son had taken the news of his imprisonment. "Just this morning, I caught him stealing in the dining room."

"No. Not my boy. He's . . . top of his class! Unless—" His shoulders fell. ". . . I wasn't very good at saving. Working for you helped take the edge off the trouble of some of my . . . vices. Gambling. You know. Got lucky too many times, got unlucky even more . . . but the boy's smart. Coulda got a job once his aunt or uncle came by to help with Loddy. I don't understand it."

Satyr nodded, worry weighing on his shoulders. Talilah should have been here by now. "I'll try to get to the bottom of it, and have it sorted by the time you're ready for them. You guys stay in the kitchen. The carriage will be here soon and won't have any interest waiting around. I'm going to check on the others." The men nodded.

Outside, the fog was still thick. The damp air made his breathing feel labored even though he walked evenly down the little road and toward the market side. She would have circled around. There wasn't a doubt in his mind that if they got caught, she would have escaped, even if she did so alone. A clattering commotion sounded back toward the inn, and his stomach dropped through his feet. He ran, a thousand possibilities whirring through his mind. Had the guards followed them back? Had Beron and the other man turn on each other? Sounds of alarm and irritation sent him through the back of the kitchen, only to have him freeze in shock.

21

Elaine

ELAINE HAD ONLY GOTTEN up for a glass of water. On one hand, she'd slept nearly the whole day. On the other, she'd been run ragged for three hours by the sudden influx of customers. And both instances meant her mouth was as dry as overcooked pork.

The stairs creaked under her as they always did, but there was no song or chatter to cover the usual sounds, so when she heard rustling in the kitchen, she smiled softly, unsurprised. Apparently, she hadn't slept too long, if Satyr was still up preparing for the morning.

The railing was sturdy and hand-worn under her palm. Every step brought her down into cooler air. The clusters of lanterns looked strange in the dark, so she hurried to the dim light in the kitchen, realizing too late that the noise had hushed to a suspicious silence.

She breezed through the door, only to come eye to eye with a haggard-looking man she'd never seen before. Her eyes flicked to the form behind him—a second man, a little farther away—and she felt the blood drain from her face as she realized there was only one reason strangers would sneak into the inn through the back door in the middle of the night.

"SATY—" her shout was muffled by the man closest to her, who lunged to press a hand over her mouth, shoving her back against the cold stove top. As she braced herself, her fingers found a smooth stone handle, and she gripped it, panic giving her the strength to shove the man away.

"Get *off* her." A vaguely familiar woman with lilac skin had raced forward from the door with a group of others in tow. She ripped the man further back with a clawed hand. As he turned to gape at the woman, Elaine swung, not sparing the male any mercy. Pain flared through her wrist, up her elbow, and into her shoulder as the stone smacked the back of his head. He hit the floor, and suddenly Elaine's arm was grappled by a strong, slender hand.

The back door slammed open, the wood smacking the stone with a resounding crack, and Elaine was ripped sideways as the impossibly strong dragonblood turned to face the newest intruder. Elaine's heart leapt in fear and in hope. Fog swept behind Satyr, his olive-tinted silhouette filling the entire doorway.

But he didn't rush forward.

The green drained from his face, leaving him ashen, and Elaine's stomach sank with it.

"She tried to call for you." The woman had clamped her arms over Elaine's, though Elaine had gone still at the familiarity in the words and the way Satyr's shoulders fell, as if he were already defeated.

His eyes were pinned to hers, but she couldn't read them beyond a sadness that was the mirror to her own. "Let her go," he said into the tense silence.

And the woman did. She obeyed, as if she'd done so a hundred times before. Elaine spun as the vise on her arms loosened, finally realizing why she seemed familiar. She was who Elaine had followed, who lurked around the inn like a specter.

She let her eyes mark every other stranger in the kitchen. Sparse clothes, sunken eyes, nervous fists clenched as if they only just resisted harming her.

"Are you okay?"

Elaine skittered sideways as Satyr's long legs brought him to her in two strides. She lifted the pan in reflex, and it trembled as her mind warred with her fear. "Who are they?" Her voice didn't shake.

He flicked his eyes around the room. "Perhaps we should speak somewhere else?"

"No." She gave the lilac-skinned woman a quick look as she shifted. "Right now."

"It's safer if you don't know."

The fear spiked into anger, into embarrassment. "And wind up surprised again?" Her voice was high and hopelessly thin. "I let it go, Satyr. I've seen her." She tossed her chin at the woman. "I've seen you meeting with people and exchanging money and it certainly didn't seem like it was for *cabbages*—but I didn't say anything. I let it go because it was none of my business and I'm going to leave anyway, and I wanted to love you while I could and I stopped myself from asking questions and then I got *attacked*." She brandished the pan at the unconscious man on the ground as her voice cracked. "*Here*." In his kitchen. Where she'd tasted what it was like to have a home again. "Why allow me to stay, and not tell me what's going on?"

"Because"—his throat bobbed as he swallowed—"I wanted to love you while I could too."

The words pierced her chest. She shook her head, and his face crumbled, like she'd shattered his heart into about a million pieces. He pinched the bridge of his nose and turned his back to the group as tromping horses and the low rumble of wagon wheels stopped outside the back door.

"I'll take care of it," the woman said, her voice gentler than Elaine would have expected. She glanced back. "Sorry for the scare."

Elaine nodded in stiff farewell, and didn't look at Satyr again until the group had gone—unconscious man included—and the carriage rumbled away.

Elaine lit a few of the sconces, banishing the unfamiliar darkness and bringing back the details of the room. There were the stacks of steins, the pots—in constant rotation because they didn't all fit on the shelf at once. There was the cutting boards, the knives. The toy creature, woven and stuffed, that sat above the icebox. She'd never asked what it was. Satyr sat on a stool, and his voice rumbled in her chest as he spoke.

"The man who took me in had already started the business when we met. He was ambitious, but as he aged, he needed more and more help to keep it going. Talilah worked with him from the beginning. Usually, she picks up the pearls, delivers them. Pays in full. I don't ask questions. But one of my men got caught. He has children." Elaine's heart caught in her throat as he went on, the words heavy with anguish. "I couldn't be responsible. We had to get him out, Elaine. They may have already lost their citizenship, the least I could do was make sure they kept their father. It's not a perfect system, but the pearls keep this place running—the inn isn't profitable on its own. I thought with time I could make it so, but hope and willpower simply haven't been enough. If I could secure the lives of Sybil and myself—make sure the inn could survive without it, I would. But I'm running at a moving target. Jimbe, the landlord, ups the price every few months, claiming there are buyers." He sighed deeply. "As if he hasn't earned well over the price of this place from me alone."

Elaine nodded, understanding settling over her alongside the weight in his voice. She lit the stove and studied him from the corner of her eye as she sourced a pot. His strong shoulders had curled under the confession, and he'd fixed his tired eyes to the floor. "It sounds like an impossible choice," she said quietly, shaving chocolate into two mugs.

"I don't mind the work," he continued slowly, as if the honesty had already damned him. "The crown's chokehold on magical components is absurd, and I have intimate knowledge of how they rake up prices for those they do allow to buy them. It's all about power. But, one day, maybe soon, I'll leave the business to someone else. The smuggling, not the inn, of course. And as for the prisoners we let out, they were petty thieves. A couple street children. We let the violent ones rot."

She nodded, stirring a spoon in each mug.

He was silent for a moment, watching her sadly. "I understand if you don't feel comfortable staying here, but I assure you it's safe. Even if I came under suspicion, I'd do anything to get you out of harm's way."

"Like you've done for others before me." That he valued life above all was obvious in the way he lived every day.

He was silent, so she turned and held his gaze until he answered.

"Yes."

She handed him the hot chocolate and set her shoulders, wanting nothing more than to smooth the worried line of his brow. She'd become quite bold recently, blurting both painful and shocking truths when she could no longer allow them to live inside her.

"I helped the princess escape."

He blinked. "What?"

She stirred the spoon in her mug. "Everyone believed she was kidnapped. But I knew her plan. I watched her pack. I held onto her bag until she needed to change so she could get out of the ball unseen. I was questioned by both Arnell's and Corsair's royalty, and threatened outright by Prince Dimitri, who was furious I didn't confess. I helped her get out. I committed treason. And I would do it again."

Satyr's lips pressed together, as if he could see where she was headed. "But what you did was *good—*"

Elaine interrupted sharply. "Everyone has their own definition of good."

She let the moment hang, shoulders set, daring him to chastise her for being reckless or secretive, as anyone else in her life would have done. A hundred arguments waited on her lips. But instead of speaking, he placed his mug down on the counter, wrapped a hand over one of her forearms and tugged her closer. Her lips trembled into a smile, and her body shuddered as she fell into him. Gentle hands threaded fingers through her hair while the other drew small circles over her back.

"I helped the princess escape too."

"What?!" Elaine clamped a hand over her mouth as the shriek echoed through the inn.

"The Wingbreaker and I are old friends. He brought her by when they needed a way out of the city. Turns out I was the right person to ask."

Elaine huffed, strangely relieved to have gotten the truth off her chest. She'd spent so long hiding it. Only to learn that she and Satyr's lives were intertwined long before she'd met him. Later she would ask how, exactly, he'd come to know Umbri's former champion. But not now. She let the warmth of him calm her frayed nerves. Benevolent criminals. Who knew?

"I'm sorry," he said into the silence that settled between them.

She sucked in a grounding breath, surrounded by his faint scent of fresh bread and snow-dusted aspen trees. "For what?"

"For scaring you. For making this place feel unwelcome."

He was good. Truly, he was. She'd never met anyone like him. Perceptive and confident, but unassuming, conscious of how he moved in the world. He hooked an arm under her and lifted, intending to bring her legs to one side, but she straddled his lap instead, heat pooling low in her belly at the way their chests pressed together.

"I wish I could stay," he murmured, sending electricity down her spine as he grazed a tusk down her neck, "but my night isn't over."

She sat back so only their legs touched, the heat of desire spinning into foreboding. "What do you mean?"

"I need to warn Beron's children the guards may be asking around, and make sure they aren't hoping his escape means he will show up. They're likely to post a guard by morning and it'll be a while before they let it up."

She wrapped her arms around his neck. "Let me go with you." His resistance was palpable, so she plowed forward, "You'll stick out less if it looks like we've just gone for an evening stroll as a couple." She placed one swift kiss on his soft lips, "It's just a quick visit." but she caught her breath as he pulled her back in. He wrapped a hand around the back of her neck, demanding, and slipped his tongue over her lips until she opened for him, and she moaned.

"Is it—time sensitive?" she asked, her spine tingling as he teased a trail of kisses down her neck.

"Yes, it's time sensitive." His low voice rumbled all the way down to her core.

"We could . . . you know . . . quickly—"

He circled her with his arms, bringing them flush and pulling her into the hardness that waited beneath his trousers. His lips grazed her ear as she hissed and rocked against him, relishing how he shifted and tightened his grip, giving her better access. "It would take the bloody Scar to stop me from doing anything except take my sweet time with you, a ghrá."

She sighed, soaking in the strength of his body.

He kissed her forehead and the grip on her loosened. "By now, the jailhouse has almost certainly realized there's been an escape. They'll spend the night organizing search parties and they'll start with the homes." His voice grew tinged with worry. "Come. You've convinced me." He grinned. "Besides, the boy doesn't like me very much. But there's no way he won't like you."

Elaine huffed a laugh. "How could he not like you?"

"I did help his dad get thrown in jail."

"And he knows that?"

"He is bright enough to suspect."

Elaine nodded. It was reason enough, though she wasn't sure how helpful she'd be.

<h1 style="text-align:center">22</h1>

Elaine

As soon as she followed him outside, clouds thwarted the already scant amount of moonlight. Cool fog licked up their ankles and washed bright colors of Arnell into shades of shadowed grey. On instinct she hesitated, fear unspooling to coil around her legs and lick up her rigid spine, but Satyr's arm was firm under her hands, and he padded along as if he could see as easily as in the sunlight. Somehow, he moved without making a sound, while she was overly conscious of the slap of her worn shoes on the cobblestone. The streets felt foreign without their regular bulk of people, but the wind was cool and ocean scented. That, at least, could ground her.

He led them through the side roads, taking a circuitous route toward the residential district. Voices carried from down the fogged street, and he threw a handout. Elaine froze, holding her breath. Moving quicker than she expected, he tucked them into a nearby alleyway. For a tense moment, they waited as torches approached, brightening the mist and then receding as their bearers walked away. Guards. Regular patrol? Or in search of escapees?

As they emerged from their hiding place, a third guard appeared, trailing the first patrol. He carried no torch, and only the darkness let Elaine leap into Satyr in time. She grappled her arms around his neck and kissed him deeply, feeling his body go soft and then hard again all at once.

"Will I need to write you two up for public indecency or are you going to find somewhere better to be?"

Elaine gave the guard a bleary-eyed look, but didn't release her hold on Satyr. "I don't see any of the public around."

"Apologies, sir." Satyr said, lifting Elaine with one arm under her back and one under her knees. "I was just about to take her home."

The guard smiled softly. She could hardly make out his sharp ears in the darkness.

"Be sure that you do. There are criminals running around tonight."

Satyr carried her past the man, who studied them until they were too far to make out in the darkness. Elaine's heart beat wildly in her chest. When he set her down, he was grinning from ear to ear and a hot blush shot up her neck and into her cheeks. "What?" she asked.

"You are a natural liar."

She sputtered. "That wasn't lying—it was acting!"

He chuckled. "Call it what you will." He kept his voice low. "I can see why the princess called on you for aid."

She smacked his arm, but she was smiling now too. "She's never seen me act out of my station. Well except once when I complained that the king was hounding us."

"Scandalous." He wiggled his eyebrows. "As soon as we get back, I expect that story in full."

She scoffed, failing miserably at feigning indignation as she wrapped both arms around one of his. Soon, their walk carried them to a prominent district, its houses large, with perfectly trimmed hedges and arched windows. Surely the merchants that lived here would have wealth set back, stipends for their children, perhaps family of similar standing. Hopefully the children in question were under the care of someone close to them.

They stopped at a tall home with white pillars that proudly supported a grand balcony above the front door. The windows were dark. No surprise, considering the time. Elaine startled as Satyr knocked, the sound echoing down the empty street. She swiveled her head back and forth until the door creaked open. A boy's tired eyes flashed, and as he went to slam it closed, Satyr shoved a hand through the crack and overpowered him.

"Get out of my house," the boy said, his voice low, "or I'll scream for the guard."

Satyr crossed his arms, keeping the toe of his boot in the door frame. Clearly the two were familiar enough for animosity. "I broke your dad out of the jailhouse."

The boy stepped back, far enough that they could enter. Satyr closed and bolted the door behind them as the young man's eyes flicked between him and Elaine.

He was tall, but his face was round with youth, his hair a greasy dark-brown that flopped unevenly to either side. His clothes were stained as well and even the inside of the house was frigid in the damp cold of the evening.

"Where's your sister?" Satyr asked.

"She's resting," the boy spat.

"She may want to hear this."

The boy's eyes grew feral. "Well, she's not going to, is she? I said she's resting."

Satyr sighed and Elaine stepped in before he could speak.

"Do you not have a caretaker here?

"No."

A thousand questions pelted through her mind, but the first that fell from her mouth was, "Have you eaten? I can whip us up something."

The boy crossed his arms in an obvious attempt to mirror Satyr. "Nothing to whip up. Where's my dad?"

Satyr stepped forward. "By now he should be—"

"Was *no one* put in charge of your care?" Elaine interrupted, the situation settling enough to stir up her frustration. The boy was young. Twelve, maybe thirteen. Not quite old enough to apprentice at the shops and certainly not old enough that most merchants would pay him a living wage for his time.

"I don't need *'caring.'*" He looked her up and down. She still wore Satyr's too-big pajamas and the ghost of a smirk tugged at his lips.

"And what about your sister?"

"I care for her. Why does it matter to you? My dad's not going to be hanged, congrats, you're both heroes. Job well done. You can go on with your lives." His fists were clenched tight. "Now can you *please* leave?"

"We were just stopping by to let you know that guards may come, asking questions, but that your father is safe, and won't be coming here." Satyr looked around. The front door opened directly into a large receiving room, too dark to make out the details. "Did he own this house?"

"I don't see how that's any of your business."

Elaine's heart clenched as Satyr's voice softened. "Because if he doesn't, someone will be expecting payments on it. Is there a close friend or family member your dad would have trusted?"

"There was." Was?

"Where are they now?"

"Gone." The boy maintained a defiant eye contact with Satyr as he spoke.

"Is that why you're thieving?" Satyr's voice hardened, rumbling with disapproval.

"I'm doing what I have to, to make sure my sister gets treatment. Gets to eat."

"It's not safe—"

Elaine cut him off, worry smothering her like a cloud. "Is she unhealthy?"

The boy's eyes flicked between them, and then to the floor. "She was born with a sugar sickness. And healers aren't cheap once the crown decides you aren't worth saving." The bitterness in his young voice made Elaine's heart ache, as did the bright red that graced his nose and the tips of his ears. "Would you allow me to at least light the fireplace?"

He shook his head. "No wood."

Satyr sighed, shifting beside her. "Once your dad is settled, I'll get you to him myself if I need to. I just wanted to let you know he's safe. You know where to find me if you need anything."

Elaine put a hand on his arm as he turned to leave. "Satyr we can't leave them here; we haven't even checked on the girl."

Satyr nodded to the boy, who stood with shoulders set like stone. "If he says she's okay, I believe him. I'll get Beron settled within the year, and things will return to normal, it's just a short break."

"A full year? With no permanent guardian?" Elaine hissed.

"Of course not. But we'll have to find whatever family Beron has left, and there's nothing we can do about it tonight. Tomorrow we'll—"

"I'm not a child!" the boy cut in, arguing in the way that only a child can. "My sister's healing has been paid for in full for a while. And I'll get a proper job once I find one she can attend."

Satyr squinted. "How did you—"

"Well, we need a wash boy!" Elaine said, barreling on through the implications and assumptions that came with saying the word 'we.' "Don't we, Satyr?"

He nodded slowly, still assessing the boy.

Elaine heaved a relieved breath but doubt lingered. "I'm not actually sure when it's best for you to start. I'll have to return to the castle in the morning, but I assume you two can work out the details?"

"You work at the castle *and* the inn?" The boy took her in again, as if trying to discern truth from a lie. "Is that why it was so busy? Because you're a castle cook?"

"Ahh—" Elaine stuttered. "No, I don't believe so."

Satyr grinned suddenly. "The boy makes a good point. If we put word out that Arnell's head royal chef was serving the city, we wouldn't have enough tables."

"Well, perhaps," she admitted. "But if I left—"

Satyr's face fell, and her stomach dropped with it. But it was true. She no longer had a home to live in. And perhaps she wanted to travel the monster infested forests or take trips to drabber, duller cities filled with stones. Old, and childless, none would be surprised if she decided an isolated cottage in one of the border villages was the best fit for her. If she stayed in Arnell she'd be staying in the inn until she found a new home—not the worst solution, but it would come with deciding she was happy to continue being party to an amount of criminal activity.

And when all was said and done there may be no reason at all to stay . . . *"There's nothing more important than family."* The words rumbled in her mind as clearly as they first time he'd said it. And family was something she couldn't give him. In a way, it would be kinder for her to leave.

A knock made her jump.

"The guards." Satyr groaned. "They're working quick lately."

"Should we hide?" Dread washed in, smothering her melancholy.

"There's a false wall under the stairs," the boy whispered, all hint of resistance gone.

Satyr pressed Elaine in the direction he'd indicated. It made sense for a smuggler to have secret nooks and crannies, though she didn't savor the idea of being stuck in a small, likely dark space with no familiarity of how it worked. A knock sounded again. Again, Satyr's steps were impossibly quiet as they moved down a wide hallway. A false door opened with a clever push mechanism and the wall swung open.

It was small. It was much too small.

"We aren't both going to fit in there." Panic seized the words in her throat so they weren't more than a squeak.

"You get in." Satyr put a warm hand around her waist. "I'll go out the back."

"They'll be waiting out the back," Elaine whispered fiercely.

"Yes, and I'll take care of them."

"So they can see who you are and start hunting for you too? Absolutely not. Get in."

"Elaine—"

"Get. In," she commanded. Down the hall, the boy opened the door.

"Don't you stupid slug breaths know what time it is? Hey—!"

Reluctantly, Satyr slipped into the space just as the guards pushed past the boy.

"Had any other visitors tonight?" one guard asked, his tone making it clear that he suspected the answer.

"We most certainly have not!" Elaine said, rounding the corner and moving back up the hall. At least the clothes she wore went along with her panicked plan. "What is the meaning of this? Forcing your way into a home in the middle of the night?"

"Apologies, miss." The man didn't sound apologetic at all. "We'll have to search the house. We've had some folk break out of jail." The guard's sash was a wrinkled powder blue, different from the castle's pristine coral.

Elaine moved to squeeze the boy's shoulders in her hands, trying to communicate that he should play along. "I don't understand. Can the crown not keep a few criminals locked away? Am I to assume Beron of all people has escaped?"

"I'm afraid I'm not at liberty to discuss it with you just yet." The man threw his chin to the two guards with him, and they moved on to search the rest of the house, their heavy boots thudding on the waxy looking wooden floor.

She kept her voice cold and even. She wouldn't allow herself to think about what might happen if they found Satyr. "Is this really necessary—"

"I'd appreciate it if you don't move from where you are, thank you," he said, cutting her off.

Elaine called after him as he moved up the stairs. "I've got another little up there, she's asleep. Try not to wake her!"

She knelt down to hug the boy. His arms stayed loose by his side. "What are your names?" she whispered.

"Trellin and Lodspur."

She pressed away but remained kneeling. "Will she be afraid?"

"Yes," he said, just as something shattered and a child's crying came from an upstairs room. Elaine was up in a flash. Two doors down, the guard stood, face pinched as he looked at the crying girl. He'd knocked a half full pitcher with his shoe. The whole upstairs was such a mess of food paper and dirty dishes that Elaine stopped short, forgetting to hide her surprise.

As the guard studied her, she swept past him, into the girl's room. She was younger than she'd expected, perhaps six or seven. "I've got you, Loddy," Elaine said, wrapping the girl in blankets and picking her up, surprised at how fragile her small frame felt under the covers. The girl continued to cry inconsolably while Elaine murmured to her. The guard inspected wardrobes and moved across the hall into the washroom. The stairs didn't creak and as soon as they made it down, Lodspur leapt out of Elaine's arms and clung to her brother, who hung onto her with his shoulders still and his chin set so resolutely Elaine's eyes watered on the spot.

Something else crashed in the kitchen. A rush of heat speared through her body, rising from the tips of her toes up into her cheeks and quite possibly into her brain, because the next thing she knew she'd marched across the hall and stormed in, filled with enough wrath to rival a dragon. "What in Atlas's bloody Scar do you think you're doing in here? Does the city guard only employ the most butterfingered, destructive, careless creatures in the kingdom? Beron isn't here. And if he came to the door I'd beat him like a rug and leave him out for leaving these kids alone with people that would fail them. Do you know I didn't know the last caretakers left until I arrived this evening? This house needs enough attention as it is, so do try to employ your limbs in a manner that does not end in me being forced to remove them."

One guard kept a straight face. "Are you threatening a member of the city guard?" A laugh burst from the man behind him.

"Well stop breaking her shit, Helio—and she won't beat you like a rug!" The man sputtered. "Oh you remind me of my mama, ma'am."

Elaine grabbed the broom to sweep the mess of cracked clay on the ground. The painted pieces reminded her of the Aspen Inn, and she felt a surge of warm fondness in spite of herself.

"Apologies," the one called Helio said, sheepish now. "We're in a hurry. And I'm clumsy on a good day."

"Oh it's all right." She sighed. "I feel protective is all. They've been through enough."

The man nodded and moved to the doorway. "Downstairs clear!" he shouted, and Elaine jumped, pressing a hand to her chest.

"I hope you guys get some rest. Ma'am." The second guard nodded his farewell with a smile.

Their orders carried down the hallway. "Set up a watch. If he comes this way, we'll know it."

The children remained by the door while Elaine followed the guards out the front. One slipped on something slick on the ground. "Looks like this fell off the pillar," he said, handing Elaine the parchment. She took it and watched as they began to search the outside of the house. When she returned inside, Trellin's eyes narrowed as he ripped the parchment from her hand and crumbled it. But she'd already seen. Her mind whirred, any plan she had kicking into overdrive.

"If you two wait for me in the kitchen, I can make you something hot to drink." She tried to keep the worry out of her voice. Trellin looped an arm around Lodspur's shoulders, seeming eager to guide her toward any distraction. As the children moved to the kitchen, Elaine cracked open the false door, and Satyr's eyebrows pinched, waiting for the explanation for the worry on her face.

"They got an eviction notice."

23

Satyr

Satyr followed Elaine to the kitchen, his eyes catching on the polished, wooden cabinet knobs and mess of bread crumbs on the counter. The children sat at a bench on one side of a heavy dinner table. "You'll need to start packing," Satyr said by way of greeting. Elaine parsed through the scant offerings in the cupboards.

"Like the bleeding Scar we will," the boy retorted, his voice rising an octave from the start of the sentence to the end.

Satyr wasn't in the mood to argue, but it seemed he'd have little choice. "You won't have much time. They'll come for the house, and then what? They'll either dump you on the street or place you in the care of some outlying farm where your father can never find you, is that what you want?"

"And where do *you* plan to take us?" the boy fired back.

"To the inn." He tried to gentle his voice. "Until we can find somewhere for you to stay. Other family. Or until Beron sends for you."

The boy wouldn't look at him. "We don't have money, if that's what you're after."

That much was clear, and it wouldn't help their situation. But it was their only option for now. "Then pay in work," Satyr said simply. "You wash dishes, clean the dining room, and in return you'll have a room or two, and a weekly allowance. You steal from my customers and you're out. Understand?"

Satyr ignored the sharp look from Elaine. She wouldn't know that he'd already caught him once at the inn. The boy held his stare for a moment before dropping his head. "Fine."

Satyr tried not to sigh in relief. It was the best deal they'd get considering the circumstances. At least they knew the goal was to be reunited with their father, in the end.

"How are we going to get out?" Elaine asked, her voice low.

"It'll have to be the morning. We can't take them now. Who knows how many patrols are out. We should stay—this house is one of the safest places to be tonight." It would be too dangerous to sneak out under the guards on watch, and it wouldn't do any good to be seen wandering again.

Elaine turned her attention on the children, her long braid swaying along her back as she passed them each a steaming mug. "So who *is* supposed to be with you?" Her tone suggested she'd have some choice words for them.

The boy pressed his lips together. The girl's leg jiggled under her chair, but her hazel eyes brightened as she warmed her hands around the hot drink. "Aunt Merry was with us at first. But there was something wrong with the house, so she left and said to talk to the house people."

"Debt, Loddy." The boy's voice was bitter.

Satyr studied him, trying to put the pieces together. They wouldn't reclaim the house unless there was a loan on it, and even then it wouldn't be until a few months had already passed. But the girl's treatment would have been taken care of by the crown while they were citizens—Beron must have been in more trouble than he let on. Even with a gambling habit, why risk getting caught smuggling if he depended on the charity of the crown for his daughter's care?

Satyr sighed, feeling the weight on his shoulders increase tenfold. Beron had admitted his vices back in the jailhouse.

What if he didn't come back?

Elaine's hand slipped into his and squeezed. The gesture filled him with warmth, then a sudden sadness, and the weight became crushing. She wouldn't stay. Not with the madness that was about to become his life.

Two children. Old enough to help, sure, but then an infant soon too. How did this happen? He couldn't support the amount of people that suddenly needed his care—

"We're going to figure it out," Elaine whispered. Satyr straightened his shoulders, his eyes flicking to the girl, Loddy, and the boy.

"What's your name?" Satyr asked. The boy refused to answer.

"His name is Trellin," Elaine chirped, clearly trying to bridge the hostility between them. "Trellin, Loddy, this is Satyr. My name is Elaine. I work in the castle kitchens and help Satyr at the inn."

"The inn?" Loddy asked.

"He works at an inn," Trellin said.

Satyr nodded. "And that's where we're going, tomorrow."

"You'll like it," Elaine said warmly. "Satyr is an excellent cook."

"As good as you?" Loddy asked. Her sandy hair was short and bedworn, with bits curling out haphazardly.

"Not by half." Satyr lifted an eyebrow.

Elaine smiled and shook her head. "That's not true."

The girl gave him a confused smile. "Then why don't *you* work at the castle?"

Satyr laughed. "I like to think of the inn as my own little castle."

She hummed thoughtfully, but launched into speaking again soon enough. "Are there other kids at the inn?"

"Not yet," he answered. "But there will be a baby born soon."

The girl seemed to remember the mug in front of her and took a sip, but her face pinched and she subtly pushed it away, but continued chatting, undeterred. "It's your baby?"

He grinned. "No. I don't have any children."

"Do you?" Loddy asked, looking at Elaine.

Elaine swept the question away with a hand. "I don't. But I think that's enough questions for now. You two should go to bed. Big day tomorrow."

Loddy opened her mouth to protest, but Trellin piped in first. "Come on, Loddy. I'll stay with you till you fall asleep."

Satyr watched the ground while they went, feeling Elaine's eyes on him, waiting until their steps faded to speak. "I don't want you to feel like you have to be involved in any of this. I'm sorry that you had to even know of it."

"I have every confidence you can handle it on your own," she said softly. "I just don't think you should have to." She tentatively reached a hand to grip his vest. "I know that it's hard that I don't have a plan. I just need to know I'm making the right choice for me. No matter what, I want you to know I'm not going anywhere until all of this is settled."

Satyr lifted a hand to her face, grazing a thumb over her impossibly soft skin. She stood on tiptoes, leaning her head toward him and a burst of happiness shot through him like fireworks as he met her in the middle, letting their foreheads rest together.

"What are you laughing about?" she asked through a smile.

"I'm happy."

"Even still?"

"I'll be happy every moment you're with me."

Satyr pushed down the rising, anticipated sadness, willing it away, compartmentalizing. He was always good at compartmentalizing.

"Would you like to be with me in bed?" she asked, her tone like a finger trailing from his neck, down his chest, over his stomach, and all the way down to—

"I very much would," he rumbled, his voice made lower by the need that grew with the invitation. "But I need to keep watch."

She leaned back. "You think they'll come back?"

"Maybe, or the kids will try to escape and tell the guards we were here—"

"—why would they—"

"I don't think they would," he said, cutting off the question. "But we—But I—need to account for all variables."

She sighed. "Alright. Well, it's been a full day, and I have to go to the castle tomorrow. I've been away too long."

"Go." He planted a kiss on her forehead. "I will make sure your sleep is uninterrupted."

"If you insist." Her eyes sparkled. Gods he loved that playful grin.

He followed her back to the stairs but stopped short. Trellin sat at the top, his back against the wall, his legs across the walkway. He opened his eyes halfway to peer at them.

"Keeping watch?" Elaine asked.

The boy nodded, looking past her and back toward Satyr, who nodded in return. Elaine turned to give him a see-you-have-more-in-common-than-you-think sort of look and ascended the stairs, stepping delicately over the boy's legs. "Goodnight, Trellin."

"Goodnight," he responded quietly.

At least he was right about the boy liking Elaine.

Satyr sat by the front door, leaning his head back against it, already missing his soft bed at home. He was due for a long nap. A series of naps.

They would make it through this night, and then he could rest.

***

Early the next morning, the kids packed. Elaine helped, making sure they took only what would fit in their room and then hastily gathered an impressive amount of garbage from the hallway upstairs.

"It would seem you two have a favorite pastry shop." The admonishment in her tone light.

"They were *sandwiches*," Trellin corrected. "Never learned to cook. Or do laundry. We had a maid but . . ."

"Well, we will fix that, won't we? What's your favorite food?"

"Fish with the crumbly breading. Not the one in the stove though."

Elaine grinned. "So fried then. That'll be dinner tonight. As soon as I get home." As Elaine turned to him, the kids gave each other an indecipherable look behind her back.

She crumbled the paper wrappings and shoved them into the sack she held. "Are you sure you're going to be alright with them by yourself?"

He snorted. "I'll be fine. I've experience with younglings, you know. In Tuskala we say it takes many to raise one. I have handled my fair share of babes, even welcomed a few as they took their first breath. Though"—he lowered his voice—"usually they've liked me."

"Give him time, I happen to believe you could win anyone over," Elaine said. Once she'd tied off the bag, she tossed it near the front door and clapped. "Alright. I'm going to work. I'll stop and send a carriage this way so you aren't trekking across town with your bags." She pressed a kiss to his cheek. "You'll be careful?"

He smoothed the worried crease in her forehead. "We will be fine. I look forward to making breaded fish with you later." He tilted her chin up to press a kiss to her lips.

"Bye everyone! Try to be careful."

As she went out the front, Satyr turned to Trellin and Loddy. "When the carriage gets here, ask the driver to take you to the traveler's market, then it's a short walk to the Aspen Inn. I drew a map"—Satyr handed him a folded parchment with streets and arrows scribbled down—"If I'm not there, ask woman named Sybil will be there, just tell her I'm on my way."

"And what are you going to do?"

"I'll have to sneak out the back, in case there are still eyes around."

"And if they catch you sneaking out?"

"Then I'll handle it."

The boy turned away to tuck the parchment into his bag. Loddy, who played on the stairs, her hair brushed now thanks to Trellin, stopped to watch their conversation with worried eyes.

She'd tucked a lute next to her bags, and Satyr made a show of admiring it. "Will you take this too?"

She shrugged. "Trellin forgot it."

The boy spoke before Satyr could. "Not much time to learn it now."

An idea took shape in Satyr's mind. He kept his voice neutral. "If you did bring it, I know someone who may be able to teach you. And customers at the inn love music."

Trellin looked at the instrument reluctantly.

"Or not," Satyr said, "it's your call. Either way."

Soon, wheels rumbled over the cobblestone. Satyr stood out of the way while the kids took their things outside and to the carriage, with Trellin carrying the burdogh's share of the bags. The driver stepped down to help them load up, and soon the carriage was rolling down the street again.

Satyr went out the back, carefully easing open the door to the fenced-in area that was overgrown compared to the meticulously pruned grass on the neighboring sides. The sun already peeked over the horizon. He cursed, thinking of Sybil. He should have had breakfast done and ready for the early risers.

He froze as a small movement caught his eye. For a brief moment, the corner of a uniformed elbow peeked into the space of the open fence gate. Steeling himself, Satyr moved on light steps toward the guard that waited beyond.

"Could I trouble you?" Satyr asked, casually. When the guard swung around the fence, he was ready. The man frowned, confused for just a moment before he went for his sword, but Satyr didn't let him draw it. He clamped a hand over the man's, trapping it against the handle of the sword, then clawed his other hand into the man's shoulder and violently slammed their heads together. As his opponent went down, Satyr wrapped him in a hug and laid him down along the inside of the fence. He spared just a moment to ensure the man was breathing well, though he slept deeply.

The city was waking as he made his way back to the inn. Once he'd made it out of the residential district, he kept to the main roads, doing his best to look like he was on his way to work—which, of course, he was. The windless day warmed quickly with the clear sky, or perhaps it was the way his blood pumped through his veins, preparing him for a chase. None came. He skirted his way into side roads as he neared the inn, just in case, mindlessly grabbing a cartwheeling scrap of butcher paper to toss when he made it back.

His shoulders lightened as he breezed through the front door. "Sybil!" Luckily only a few regulars sat nursing their tea.

"Where have you been?!" she all but shrieked as she moved from behind the counter. He motioned for her to follow him to the kitchen. She sat on the stool near the ovens, groaning. "I thought I was going to have to run this place without you." Her eyes had dark bags under them, her face wan.

He went for the mugs, pouring a glass of water and passing it to her. "I'm sorry. We got held up unexpectedly. I should have been here."

"Is Elaine not with you? I understand the two of you need space, but I had to make toasted bread and fruit for breakfast, I think they certainly noticed your absence."

Satyr could feel a blush darken his cheeks and the insinuation, but over explaining wouldn't do Sybil any good. "She went to the castle this morning, for work."

"Well," Sybil wiped her head with a damp towel that hung on her apron. "I'm glad she's feeling better."

Satyr pulled his brow together softly, feigning ignorance. "Better?"

Sybil scoffed, moving to dump two half full mugs from one side of the sink and then plunked them into the soapy water in the other. "Yes. Better. You aren't the only one who notices things."

Satyr smiled. "Sometimes I forget that not everything I know is a well-kept secret. Have you seen Talilah?" He peeked out the back door, propping it with a rock for the sake of airflow.

She shrugged, scrubbing at the dishes. "No, no one has really been in yet."

That made sense. It was still early. Earlier than he'd realized. He scooted beside her, angling his body so he could look at her face. Wisps of hair curled around her temples "Can you do me a favor?"

Sybil narrowed her eyes at him. They both knew what he was about to say.

"Will you rest in bed until dinner?"

Her eyebrows rose into her hairline. "I am perfectly happy to work, it really hasn't been that harrowing. We've had maybe three fishermen come in." She turned back to her task, dismissing him.

Perhaps he could bargain with her. "Okay, then can you do me two favors?"

She scoffed again, but didn't look at him this time.

He plowed on. "Will you please, *please* let me make us breakfast, and *then* will you rest in bed until dinner? We don't know how busy it will get tonight."

"Satyr, I'm fine. I can work. My hands are as good as any, and you need the help."

She was right, but if they had another rush this evening they wouldn't have the option to sit and rest. "You look exhausted."

She slung a wet fist to her hip. "You flatter me, orc. It may surprise you, but growing a babe is exhausting. I'm not going to lay in bed all day. I'd rather have aching feet than be intolerably bored."

He sighed. She'd finished the dishes, and he raced her to the water pitcher, snatching and refilling them before she could and offering her indignant expression a wicked grin. "Fine, then will you take a chair out front and call for me if a couple children walk in?"

She sighed and walked out, through the dining room, and out the front door—without grabbing a chair.

He chuckled, tossed some sausages in a pot, and got started with a roux for the gravy, pleased to settle back into the routine—for now.

Sybil walked back in only a few minutes later. "They're here."

He nodded. "Will you stir this? For just a moment. Here—" He tucked the stool beneath her, and she sighed as he reached over her, tossing the sausages around one more time. "And if these start to smell burned, will you flip them?"

She lifted the spatula like a stone soldier, choosing not to dignify his over explaining with a response.

He rushed into the dining room, tossing a wave and a "fáilte!" at a customer that greeted him. Loddy stood wide eyed behind Trellin, whose ruddy face betrayed the weight of the bags at his feet. He straightened as Satyr approached.

"So this is *your* inn?" Loddy asked before Satyr had figured out what to say. Her eyes dazzled in the soft light of the paper lanterns.

"Yep," he waved an arm toward the mostly empty tables. "Why don't you two have a seat and I'll take your bags up to your rooms."

"Room," Trellin corrected.

"Room," Satyr said, nodding as he scooped up their things. He would need to rearrange a couple beds, then. It made sense the boy wouldn't want them separated, and they could always change rooms in the future. Plus, enough travelers came and went that he'd need to make sure they had a heavy duty lock as well.

Satyr sighed as he went up the stairs.

After he'd put their bags in the room beside his, he trotted down to find Sybil chatting with the children.

"Water, and what else can I get for you?" she asked.

"She needs to avoid sugar," Satyr said, moving next to them quickly.

Sybil nodded, tipping her head to Trellin. "This young man right here was just saying that."

"Yes I can!" Loddy argued. "Sometimes."

Trellin nodded. "The healer's visits help the sugar sickness for a while, but it wears off over time."

Sybil looked back at him, her brow pinched in silent question.

He shook his head, hoping to convey with his eyes that he'd explain later. "I don't think that will be a problem."

Loddy sat back in her chair. "Daddy always let me have sugar after the visits."

Satyr nodded. "I think that makes sense, but we will have to make sure the healer agrees before we make any decisions. When is your next visit?"

Loddy looked to Trellin.

"Three weeks," he said.

"And how will the healer know where to find you?"

"We go to him. And like I said we are paid in full for the year."

Satyr couldn't help the rumble of suspicion in his voice. "And where did you get that kind of coin?"

"However I had to," the boy said, his eyes like iron.

Satyr regarded him for a moment. "You're a good kid. Your father would be proud."

24

Elaine

ELAINE HAD NEVER SEEN the morning streets so crowded. Carriages rolled down the main thoroughfare, their wood-on-stone rumbling akin to thunder. She shuffled past the groups that studded the walkway. A family with children walked with wrapped pastries in hand, the mother scooping jelly off the smallest one's cheeks. Farther down, a woman wept, her quiet sobs dying on the damp, salty air. Elaine's stomach flipped as she noted the red on her skirts was not a design, but a darkened stain. Monster attacks weren't uncommon outside the protection of the villages' lawstones, but the safety, and optimism, made it easy to forget.

She nodded to the guards as she passed into the castle courtyard, and made her way through the kitchen garden, plucking a bit of peppermint to chew.

"Elaine!" Isobel said as she pushed open the door. "Thank the gods you're here. First the rations and now the festival. It seems I haven't stopped moving for an entire week!"

"I'm sorry." Elaine offered an apologetic smile as she tied on a clean white apron. "Did you get my message?"

"Yes. How are you feeling now?"

Elaine poured herself a mug of tea from a lukewarm pot, letting the act distract her. How was she feeling? Guilty. She'd all but forgotten about her father's death, too obsessed with the changes in her life and the metaphorical fires that had needed dousing. She hadn't told Satyr that the house had sold, or that she had yet to make a decision. "Ready to work," she said before pressing forward. "How has it been here?"

"Fine." The fae woman shrugged. "I mean. Busy. Absurdly busy. And there's only more to do. Are you sure you're okay?"

Elaine resisted the urge to smooth down her hair or wipe her tired eyes. "I was unwell. For longer than expected." Airam breezed out of the pantry, holding a clipboard. "How do our supplies look?" Elaine asked.

"Terrible. We weren't given nearly enough time to do a proper restock." He clapped his hands, his face split in half with a wicked grin. "Just another reason we're glad you're back. What shall we prep today?"

Breakfast came and went in a flurry, and once lunch was prepped, she excused herself, carrying a tray of puff pastries and lavender chamomile tea on a tray up the servant's stairwell.

Leo's new guard, a handsome, midnight-skinned human man, bowed to her unnecessarily. "Did the princess call for you?"

"No," Elaine said plainly, emboldened by his smile. "Still, I think if you ask her if she'd like some tea, she'd happily accept."

The guard nodded and knocked.

From beyond, Leo called for him to open the door and he ushered Elaine inside. The princess's eyes brightened, and she flew off her bed to embrace Elaine, and the guard was good enough to take the tray as she stumbled under the strength of the shorter woman's affection.

"Elaine! I feel as though I've hardly seen you lately."

Elaine straightened her skirts. "I was unwell."

Leo brushed a light hand over her cheek. "You don't look unwell—you almost look . . . brighter."

Elaine felt herself redden under the scrutiny. She didn't consider herself to be shy when it came down to it, but she was certainly easily embarrassed, and it compounded with the guilt that wove its way through her again. She *did* feel brighter, or perhaps lighter. Like she might hope again.

The princess studied her, and Elaine wondered if she somehow betrayed the warring emotions. But Leo only gestured to the overstuffed bed. "You're welcome to sit."

Elaine remained standing, though there was also a sofa and the seat before the tall vanity, which spilled over with a hodgepodge of books and jewelry. "How are *you* doing?" she asked. After only a few weeks, remarkably little was whispered about the princess, her apparent kidnapping, and the chaos that erupted upon her return. It seemed the city had been eager to turn its attention to the coming summer, and the surprise festival. No doubt that had been partly why the king announced it at all.

Leo huffed, sinking onto her bed, ruffling the fabric of a simple, but finely made purple gown. "I'm well. Everything is back to normal." She smiled, her eyes suddenly tired now too. But she didn't let the moment linger. "Now I insist, sit. Have one of these—what are these? They look incredible."

"They're the same puff pastries; I just stuffed and drizzled them with a creamed chocolate." A specialty of the Aspen Inn she'd perfected, if only to see one of Satyr's surprised smiles.

"Ohmygods," Leo said, having taken a bite and draped a hand over her full mouth. "They're incredible. Come, sit, you must have one!"

Elaine relented. It always felt strange to talk to the princess in her room as if she were her closest friend. She was, in a way, but she was also royalty, and the disconnect in her mind meant she had a hard time processing the shifting boundaries between them. Seymour had always been strict with propriety, respecting station, both bitter and admiring of those of higher class. They'd been well enough off, to be sure. He worked as a merchant and Elaine worked at the castle, though he'd always chastised her when she spoke of Leo as if she were a friend.

It was absurd, really. For years, the princess had encouraged her, reaching a hand out over and over again. Stubborn. All but prying information from her over the years. How she'd fought to have a family, and failed over and over. How in the end it meant she was left even more alone than before.

Elaine laid back on the bed, letting her breath come out in a woosh. Leo grinned and fell back too.

"I like your hair. I should have said so before." Elaine wouldn't allow anymore silliness keep distance between them.

"We were both a bit concerned with other matters, I believe."

The windows cast streaks of light over the painted ceiling.

"My father died."

Leo sucked in a breath. "Gods, Elaine—"

"And I sold my house." Never in her life did she think she'd interrupt a princess.

Leo didn't seem to notice, instead facing her, her scarlet hair just brushing her chin as she rolled to her side. "You're leaving?" The question was quiet.

"I . . . I don't know. But the house is *gone*," Elaine said, relief crashing into her all at once and spilling over her face in quiet tears. "And I feel horrid that I'm happier now than I have been for years. I just needed a reason to let it go. I needed a reason to let it all go."

Leo went quiet. After a moment she looked away, staring up at the ceiling with Elaine before she spoke again.

"I'm sure he would have been glad to be the reason."

Elaine had hoped to feel better once she returned to work. As it was, her mind refused to settle, swirling around Satyr and the inn. The children and Sybil. In the background loomed the fact of her homelessness and the decision she needed to make. If she stayed, she knew she'd throw herself into the responsibility that waited at the inn. And if she left, she'd be away from this city, away from everything that connected her to the life she desperately needed to escape.

She could start over. Maybe even open her own shop a few towns over. She'd still be able to visit. The thought didn't settle well. She'd always fancied the idea of a shop of her own, but the castle offered a unique combination of control and structure. The boy had been right that if the city learned the castle head chef cooked at the Aspen Inn, the curious would flock to it. And once the tide began, word of mouth would turn it into a wave. And with she and Satyr's skills combined, they might have a shot at making a profit after enough time.

If she chose to stay. In Arnell. With Satyr—perhaps she could buy a different house, perhaps she could continue to work at the castle, but her heart would remain hopelessly tangled. If she stayed, she would share the responsibilities he carried.

And it had been merely *weeks* since she'd met any of them.

She loved him. And in a vacuum, there would be no contest. But the added complication of fostering children, of sharing a life with all four—soon to be five—of them. Did she want to be a smuggler? A life raft for a struggling inn?

Satyr wouldn't blame her for choosing herself. Would likely encourage it.

She walked back in a haze. The sun was a little later to set each day, so the clatter of the city retired later each night. The air smelled of sweet salt and her soft shoes let her feet feel every break and chip in the cobblestone. Yet again, she promised herself she'd stop at the shops to get new ones soon. Once everything was settled.

If she was to leave, she would have to wait until Sybil had her baby. Sure, she could leave money behind to pay for the healer, but there was no way of knowing how the birth would go. If there would be care needed after. She should stay. At least for a little while longer.

When she made it back to the inn, Trellin was cleaning tables while Loddy animatedly chatted with an older couple that seemed charmed by her questions. Satyr met her at the kitchen doorway, wrapping his arms around her and burying his face in her neck. He squeezed and breathed deep, walking backwards to lead her into the back.

"You okay?"

"Just enjoying you." He gently trailed a tusk up her neck.

She grinned, sinking into him. "Mmmm. What was for dinner?"

"Just a duck with a honey maple glaze." He was so close the words danced over her skin.

"With the Nasturtiums?" she said, unable to hide her surprise.

He pulled back to pin her with his gaze, eyes flashing. "What can I say, you're a bad influence. How was your day?"

"It was good," she answered automatically. "Well, it was hectic. Oh! I forgot, I should get getting the plants from the house delivered here soon, I hope that's okay?"

He squeezed. "Of course it's okay. Though if memory serves, there may be more than will fit in your room's window. You're welcome to use the one's downstairs too."

She smiled. "It would make it very green."

"It wouldn't be the only thing."

She snorted. Where's Sybil?"

He kept one arm around her and lifted the other away to stir a sizzling pan. "She seemed tired, so I sent her up early. Besides, Trellin needs to stay busy or his hands might start to wander."

Elaine swatted his shoulder but didn't pull away. "You shouldn't be so hard on him."

Satyr grinned, but his face turned serious. "He's floundering. He'll feel better with someone else in charge. Someone he can trust."

The young man in question came back and dumped dishes in the sink.

"Good evening, Trellin," Elaine trilled, stepping out of Satyr's hold.

The boy turned and, instead of speaking, he smirked and gave her a dramatic, clumsy bow. When he'd gone back out the door, Elaine looked to Satyr in question.

He stretched his arms up and scratched the back of his head as he spoke. "I may have expressed the importance of being polite to the customers. And to you. It seems he's taken it as some kind of challenge."

Elaine blinked, and shook her head, her confused smile falling away as reality swept in like the tide. "Do you have any idea when Beron might get in touch with you?"

She almost regretted asking, with the way worry clouded the playful mood. "None," he said.

She spoke slowly, trying and failing not to add her own concern to what already weighed on him. "But you're sure you'll hear from him soon?"

His shoulders sagged. "No. The man was a gambler. And in more debt than he let on. It seems they were on the verge of losing their house, no matter that he got arrested."

Elaine followed his train of thought. "So then whatever family member came to inherit the kids found no money, just assets that had already been depleted."

He nodded. "I told him to contact me when he was ready for me to get the children to him."

"But for now," Elaine whispered.

"For now," he said, following her gaze to the dining room.

The dinner rush was as busy as the night before, and once they'd prepped breakfast and the dining room closed, the children helped Satyr clean up while Elaine went upstairs with aching feet. In her room, she found the pajamas Satyr had gifted her, washed, folded, and waiting on her bed. She smiled, brushing a finger over the fabric.

"Elaine?" Sybil stood at the door, leaning against the door frame. Her long hair was down, and her bare feet and shins peeked out beneath a long sleep shirt.

"Hey," Elaine said, "you okay?"

"Yeah. I—" She winced, holding her belly.

Elaine's heart leapt into overdrive as she moved to the door. "Is the baby coming?"

Sybil sucked in air through pursed lips and sighed, her body relaxing. "No. No, I don't think so. I think it's the same as last time. False labor. But my back aches."

Elaine ushered the woman to her bed and lit a candle. "Well, come, let me get some extra pillows. I can ask Satyr for extra blankets too? Or I could go grab yours I suppose. Are you cold? Do you need water?"

Sybil's almond eyes betrayed her exhaustion, but she smiled warmly. "No. I just didn't want to be alone. Just in case. Is that okay?"

Elaine swept the edge of the blanket down in invitation. "Is it okay—I insist!" She patted the sheet. "The healer said to lay down on your left side, right? Let me get you some water. I promise I'll be right back up."

Elaine spirited down the hallway and Satyr met her on the stairs. He caught her with a finger under her chin, lifting her face to his. "Everything okay?"

She hadn't realized how short of breath she was. Her heart seemed convinced she'd need to leap into action at any moment. "Yes, I'm just getting Sybil some water. She's going to lay with me tonight."

He studied her for a moment, his deep-olive colored skin made darker by the shadowy stairway. "If you need me, you may have to come in the room to get me up. And if it's time, wake me as soon as you know." A smile split his face, so fierce she couldn't help but smile back. "A babe born in a Tuskalan inn deserves a proper Tuskalan welcome."

Elaine chuckled, popping up on her toes to plant a quick kiss on his lips. "I'm sure we will be okay. She said it feels the same as before. If it doesn't stop, we will just have to call the healer in."

Satyr nodded and just as she turned to walk away, he hooked an arm around her waist. "I'll be thinking of you," he said, peppering kisses down her neck. She arched into him, heat immediately blossoming deep in her belly. "Oh dear gods, you're perfect," he whispered as he let one hand fall to grip her backside. Her brain emptied and she nearly dropped the clay cup of water. She couldn't help a groan. Suddenly, he pulled back, grinning. "Don't let me distract you." The words were a challenge.

"I absolutely want you to distract me." But Sybil didn't want to be alone. And Elaine had promised she'd be right back. "Tomorrow?"

"Tomorrow," he growled, sending shivers down to the tips of her toes.

She floated up the stairs. Sybil laid on her side, a pillow between her legs.

"I'll set this here." Elaine placed the water on the nightstand. "Is it still happening?"

Sybil nodded, keeping her eyes closed. Elaine took the opportunity to quickly shimmy out of her dress and into the pajamas. Only the moon lit the room as she blew out the candle and laid down in the bed, briefly registering that it was too small to fit them both without touching. After a moment, Sybil sucked in a breath.

"You okay?"

It took her a moment to answer. "Yes. It's not too bad. Really, it's my legs. I think I pushed myself too hard today. They've never hurt like this before though."

"Do you think the baby is pressing down on your hips?"

"Oh the baby is definitely crushing everything that's in its way. I can hardly breathe let alone cough and not worry about peeing myself."

Elaine snorted. "It sounds terrible."

"It's alright. Truly I'm not sure I was meant to be a glowing, radiantly pregnant woman. It seems I'm much more like a troll."

Elaine scoffed even as she grinned at Sybil's back. "Don't say that! You're perfectly radiant. People can't take their eyes off you."

"Yes. I imagine it's all the waddling."

Elaine laughed again, but Sybil sucked in another breath.

"Was that one quicker than the last?" Elaine had little experience with childbirth herself, but knew about as much as any woman was taught: They should count. If the contractions kept getting closer together, that meant the baby was on its way.

"Maybe. It's been happening a while. But it could be wishful thinking."

Elaine turned so they were back to back. "If it's just cramps from overwork, the water might help."

Sybil sat up halfway and reached for the water. Elaine curled the blankets in her fist, tucking them up to her chin. She worried to herself, but even if the child decided it was time, they wouldn't need to call for the healer until the end. Towels were in the kitchen pantry, blankets in the hallway cupboard.

Sybil tensed again.

Elaine started counting.

25

Elaine

Sybil groaned into a pillow as Elaine massaged her back. The contractions had grown closer until her waters broke and then everything seemed to rush by in a gallop. Despite claiming to be a deep sleeper, Satyr woke and rushed for the healer at the first cry she couldn't bite back. The commotion drew Trellin and Loddy, and Elaine had no idea what the healer would need, but she sent them for blankets, and towels, both wet and dry, if only to keep them busy.

The healer arrived in his own pajamas and sleepily waved them all out the door. Elaine fell into Satyr, the joints of her fingers angry for her efforts. He wrapped her up in his arms and set his chin on her head.

"Is she going to be okay?" asked Loddy from the doorway of their room.

"Of course she is," Trellin said quickly. "She has the healer with her."

Satyr swayed as he held her. She'd been up for hours already, but she didn't feel the least bit tired. Her heart hadn't slowed for a moment.

"Are you guys hungry for breakfast?" Elaine asked. It may be a while yet before everything was said and done. And Sybil's cries echoed down the doorway.

Before anyone answered, the healer poked his head out. "The child is close." He looked to Elaine. "She asked for you."

Elaine's stomach plummeted to the floor. She'd never been part of a birth before. And she'd only ever felt dashed hopes and bitterness about her own body's inability. Helping Sybil through the labor was one thing. But being there for the birth . . . Sybil deserved to have someone who was not conflicted, who was unabashedly excited.

What if Elaine could not help her selfishness? What if she allowed her years of grief to color the day?

What a loss it would be for this woman she'd grown to adore and admire, if Elaine was not all she needed her to be in this moment.

Satyr kissed her forehead. "She's lucky to have you here."

She looked at him, unable to hide the fear on her face or the tears in her eyes.

A line formed between his brow as he studied her. And then, as if he'd come to some decision, he gripped her face with both hands, and his eyes went soft with a vulnerable intensity. "I love you."

Elaine felt something inside of her crumble at last. A dam, it seemed, as everything flooded in at once: years of disappointment, the anger she'd bit down on for so long, the guilt she felt then and now, the fear of what she had no choice now but to say aloud, hope for the same, and gratefulness for the weeks of joy, the simple, lifesaving joy that she hadn't had for years of her life, but that she would cherish forever. Beyond the door, Sybil cried out in pain. She needed Elaine—she hadn't wanted to be alone.

"I love you too." Her voice broke. "But—" Her heart ached as Satyr stilled, like he was preparing for a blow. "I can't have children," she whispered. He blinked, his mouth falling open as he tried to process the words. She barreled through the words. "And I know you want family—"

"I *have* a family," he said with conviction. He touched his forehead to hers. "I have every person that has graced this inn. I have Thorin, Percy, and Kelre. Talilah. Sybil, and this child—Trellin and Loddy. I want *you*." He pressed a heartbreakingly gentle kiss to her lips. "Only you."

Sybil's cries pierced through the door, this time alongside the healer's shouts. "Anyone that wants to be in here better come now!"

Elaine allowed herself a single, laughing gasp before she nodded, pulling out of his arms and wiping her eyes to stop their watering. She paused to look back as she wrapped a hand over the doorknob, but whatever she was going to say was lost in the enormity of what she needed to do. Instead, she took a fortifying breath, and Satyr nodded, without a shred of doubt. And his confidence carried her across the threshold.

The room was lit by a few lanterns now, and the healer knelt on the floor, rustling through the bag he brought.

Sybil's face was screwed tight, her body tense. Her hair hung in thick, damp clumps.

Five strides had Elaine's mind narrowed to needle point focus. "Hey, hey, take a deep breath, breathe with me," she said, taking Sybil's hand. The woman squeezed, her grip like fire.

"Sit behind her," the healer ordered without preamble.

Elaine could hardly hear him from where he knelt on the floor. "What?"

"Get behind her, sitting up on your knees. She's going to use you as a brace."

Elaine did as instructed, grateful to be in pants as she struggled against the softness of the mattress.

"Okay, Sybil." The healer spoke loudly. Sit up a bit—yes, tuck your feet under you—I have this"—he produced a firm, square pillow from the floor beside him—"so you don't have to balance." His voice lowered again, addressing Elaine. "Now you keep your hands under her arms."

Elaine leaned into her friend, acting as a counterbalance as she relaxed. The room grew sweltering, but Elaine breathed deeply and intentionally, quietly hoping Sybil would fall into the same pattern.

"Alright, Sybil," the healer said. "It's time. When the next one comes, follow your body's lead."

Not a moment later, Sybyl went rigid again, her knuckles going white as she steeled herself against the pain. Elaine implored her to breathe.

"Here we go—go go go—yes!" the man's voice rose into a shout. "Okay! One more time! Just one more time."

Sybil's body curled with the force of another contraction, and Elaine fought to steady her with burning legs and slick hands. She braced her aching arms as Sybil bared down again and all at once Elaine's heart went suddenly steady—

If she stayed in Arnell, she could leave. If she left, she could return. She'd made mistakes. She'd had her life fall apart spectacularly, and she'd survived. She'd *lived.* After years of living in the shadow of her looming expectations, she'd emerged alone, with nothing to show for soldiering through, and still she laughed. Still she found unapologetic joy. On the other side of the gut churning shame and shattered wishes, there was hope. There was kindness and love and—they were going to be okay. All of them. Sybil and the baby. Trellin and Loddy. Elaine and Satyr. They'd figure it out.

Together.

As Sybil relaxed again, the healer's hands moved in a flurry. Elaine's stomach dropped through the floor as he looked at the baby, his brow creased.

"Is it over?" Sybil asked, dazed.

It couldn't be over.

The man's hands moved frantically. The room was silent.

"What's wrong?" Elaine's heart redoubled its efforts as the man ignored her in favor of the quiet bundle in his arms.

Sybil sagged over, her head falling sideways and back into Elaine's chest. Her eyes were closed. "Sybil?" She shook her shoulders. "Wait"—Elaine leapt out of the bed—"she's unconscious!"

"Godsdamn it!" The healer all but threw the tiny babe at her. "Rub his arms and legs!" His hands glowed as he worked over the unconscious mother.

Satyr appeared in the doorway, his face tight with worry.

Elaine frantically rubbed the towel over the baby's skin. "He's not breathing!"

"To me," Satyr said, his face a mask of calm.

The healer shook his head sadly as Elaine handed the baby over without question. The orc let the towel fall and braced the child's back, careful to cradle his head and neck as he lifted him up and away. Then he grinned. Fierce and sudden—"*Fáilte!*" he shouted, in that booming voice that cut through busy inns and empty homes.

As one, the room startled.

Sybil's eyes shot open.

And the infant began to cry.

26

Elaine

SYBIL KEPT THE BABE close to her skin. He slept peacefully on her chest, his pointed ears so tiny, his little lips suckling in his sleep.

"I think everything is settled here," the healer told Elaine quietly.

She nodded, and squeezed Sybil's hand. "Shall I bring you some breakfast?"

The woman smiled. Her hair was mussed and frizzed, her eyes betrayed the monumental task her body had overcome, and her smile was indescribably radiant. "Please. Tell Satyr I'll need a double portion."

Elaine laughed. "He'll be glad to hear it."

She met the healer at the door. "Let me walk you out." She would need to make sure he got his money. He'd crowed in victory when the babe came to, his eyes shining bright. In that moment, Elaine decided that she rather liked the man, despite his rough demeanor. She grabbed her coin purse and followed him down the steps and into the dining room. Satyr stood behind the counter. His eyes were cradled by dark half-moons, but he gave them a sleepy smile.

"Let me wrap something for you," he said, and then disappeared into the back.

The man settled into a chair and Elaine's coin purse jingled as she sidled next to him, fiddling with the knot. "Now I wasn't sure when the babe would come so I only carried a bit extra around. If it's more than I have here, we can walk down to the bank together."

The man shook his head. "You don't have to pay me." Wrinkles marred his grey pajamas at the wrists and elbows. His hair was flat on one side and stuck up oddly on the other.

"Sybil isn't an Arnell citizen," Elaine reminded him.

His eyes shone again and the exhaustion seemed to leave his face as he smiled. "I know. But this job"—he shrugged—"it's all wounds and fear. Illness. Death. It isn't every day I get to bring life into this world. And there are things more precious than gold. Use it to feed the mother, clothe the child. In fact, give it to her and let her decide."

Satyr reappeared, carrying something warm wrapped in paper. The healer's eyes caught and followed him. "I wish I were as personable as you. But alas, I am cursed to be surly."

Satyr slid the meal toward him, leaning his crossed arms on the counter. "We feed the personable and the surly. If you ever find yourself in need of a meal, you'll find one here, no questions asked."

The healer nodded, clearing his throat as if clinging to composure despite his ruffled appearance. "Yes. Well. Thank you. I'll be off then. Call for me if there's any further trouble." He stood from his chair, but paused. "Actually, I must ask what you said to the babe. I'm afraid wondering forever may drive me mad."

Satyr chuckled. "*Fáilte.* Welcome! It is how orcs in Tuskala are greeted into this world, and it is how we believe we will be greeted in the next."

The man nodded slowly, a smile tugging at one side of his mouth. As the door closed behind him, Elaine looked to Satyr.

"Well," he said. "That was more excitement than I ever wanted in my lifetime. I'd rather fight ten balverines. A hundred balverines!"

She'd stand no chance against a balverine, but she smiled, nodding in agreement. "Shall I make some tea?"

He cupped her hand with his own. "It's already brewing."

She gently traced her thumb around the scabs on his knuckles. "Did the children eat?"

"They did, but I sent them back up. Trellin was asleep on his feet."

Elaine huffed a laugh. "I could use a nap myself."

"Well, go! Rest."

"At least let me help you light the candles. The sun will be up soon. Our breakfast regulars will arrive, and I may as well get dressed today and go to the castle."

"You're going today?"

Sybil may need help, but if all went well, both she and the babe would sleep. "Did you want me to stay?"

"You know that I want you to stay," he said softly.

The words jolted her out of exhaustion.

He continued slowly, his eyes vulnerable and tired. "I'm not asking you to live in the inn, or even be involved here at all if it's too much. I'm asking you to stay in Arnell. With me. Stay with me, Elaine. I know that it's selfish but—"

Elaine all but leapt over the counter to kiss him. His shirt was soft in her hands as she yanked him down so she could reach his lips. In an instant, he'd curled his arms around her back and lifted, putting her on her knees on the counter. His hands, gods his hands. They found her backside, propping her up and bringing her closer. She squealed as he stepped back, pulling her legs around him and walking to the kitchen. The kiss remained unbroken as he walked to the pantry—and then pressed a false door open.

She paused then, taking in the hidden space. It was much larger than the one in Beron's house. Shelves lined the bottom, empty but for a small box high up.

"I shouldn't be surprised." She clung tight as he leapt up the stairs that led to a loft above.

He hadn't missed a beat, only sat her on the edge of a tall, naked bed and dragged his tongue down her neck. "You shouldn't," he agreed.

Fire followed in the wake of his lips. His fingers caressed the hem of the pajama shirt, slowly raising it. "Do you know what it does to me, every godsdamn time I see you wearing this?"

His voice rumbled through her chest, and she grinned. "Wearing an oversized shirt?"

"Wearing what's *mine*," he said, twisting the fabric in his fist just tight enough she knew the word was intentional. Her heart fluttered even as sensation blazed in her core. "You're the only one I've given everything to." She could feel his desire fighting to free itself from the bind of his trousers. "You're the only one who knows all of me. Who I don't have to hide from, in one way or another." She moaned as he nipped at her neck.

"*All* of you?" The words were a challenge. She cupped a hand over his trousers, massaging as well as she could through his clothes.

He grinned and flicked her wrist up over her head, wrestling her pajama shirt off at the same time. Once she was free, he braced his hands on either side of her face and captured her mouth with his. The barest friction of his body on her chest had her aching. The knot of his trousers resisted for only a moment before she had it loose and they puddled to the floor. He stepped back and slipped his shirt up and off, revealing a latticework of scars.

Her insides buzzed with anticipation as he paused, studying her as she studied him. His body was thick and strong. His arms had always been impressive, but seeing the entirety of him gave her a sudden appreciation for his power. It stayed dormant behind a personable smile and a love of food, but now, in the dim light, the shadows and highlights made her feel like she saw the warrior that lived beneath.

Slowly, deliberately, he hooked his thumbs beneath his underclothes and tugged them down, letting the full length of him spring free.

Elaine dropped to her knees, taking him in both hands. She looked up to watch his face as she began dragging her tongue in circles over the beads of wetness that waited for her at its tip.

He groaned, tangling his fingers in her messy, braided hair. "Elaine," he rumbled.

"Hmm?" She teased over him, her tongue exploring his impressive girth.

"I haven't even gotten your clothes off," he objected.

She let her lips pop as she pulled back.

"And what would you do once you'd gotten my clothes off?" Her jaw stretched as she went back to work, trying to take him further.

"I would . . ." he sighed and grew ever firmer against her tongue. "I would let my mouth trail every inch of you. I would find what made you beg and I would do it over and over again. And once you were ready, I'd sink every part of me into you, and hope the impression I left made you ache to have me again."

Elaine moaned again, a hollow need spurring her on. His fist tightened in her hair, but instead of guiding her further onto him, he pulled her up. She stood, tugging the waist of her sleep pants down and letting them fall as he smoothed his hands from her neck, over her shoulders, down her arms, and clasped each of her wrists into one of his.

"You're so perfect," he murmured, lifting her arms over her head and backing her into the bed until her knees buckled. He followed her down, settling on her chest so his voice vibrated every inch of her. "I've pictured this every day since the moment I met you. But you're more beautiful than I could have imagined." He pressed her hands back, pinning them over her head. "I'm going to take my time getting you ready for me."

He touched his forehead to hers as he trailed a finger down her neck and front. "Alas, you can't be too loud. These walls are hidden, but thin." She laughed then groaned as he spread her with two fingers, and dipped a third into her wetness, trailing it up and around the sensitive space between her legs.

"Satyr," she breathed, seeking more friction with her hips, trying to wrap her legs around him. Trying to free her hands so she could touch him too.

"Is that the spot, a ghrá?" Rather than waiting on her answer, he dipped his head down and captured her nipple in his mouth, gently swirling his tongue, giving her a distinct image of what his mouth could do as his fingers moved in tandem. She bit down on a cry as he dipped his fingers into her further, and she felt more than heard the satisfied rumble in his chest.

"So eager," he said, but she could only whine her need for more. He released her hands as he knelt, instead propping her leg up over his shoulder, keeping her braced as he spread her knees apart. His fingers curled inside her as he lowered his head and explored with his tongue.

"Oh, gods." She gripped his hair and threw her head back as he worked her, keeping a steady rhythm. The heat built in agonizing waves, and she wasn't above begging for mercy.

"Satyr, I need you."

He pulled back for only a moment. "You have me, a ghrá." He didn't waver, he didn't drive into a frenzy with his tongue to convince her of his enthusiasm. He worshiped her. Slowly. Intentionally.

"Satyr, please." She was so close now. Her entire body stood at the edge. Still, he kept on, unhurried, lingering, driving the intensity further. Just when she thought he would give in to her pleas he pulled back.

"You're flooded, a ghrá. I need to feel you when you shatter for me." He shifted his weight over her, and she curled her legs around him, pressing them closer together. "If you are ready?" he murmured.

She nodded, breath heaving. She was ready. More than ready. "Please."

He positioned himself and pressed in, just a little at first.

"Oh gods," she said, curling her hips up to take more.

"I don't want to hurt you." He kept his body rigidly still.

"You won't." His back was warm as she curled her legs around him, using the leverage to bring them closer.

He groaned, the sound rumbling through her chest. She worked herself down until he finally, blessedly settled his hips, fully seating himself inside her. Her breath came in quick gasps, but she relished the way he stretched her.

"Is it too much?"

"No." Her voice was hardly more than a pant. "Don't stop, please."

His voice was filled with doubt. "You're so tight, Elaine. We should let you adjust."

"It will only take a moment. Would you feel better if I was on top?"

He nuzzled her neck, sending hot sparks shooting down her spine. "Will you be careful with yourself if you're on top?"

"Careful is . . . a word."

His laugh rumbled through her, and her hips sought friction against him. Relenting, he curled an arm beneath her before turning them, putting his back to the bed and leaving her straddled on top.

"Oh, thank you," she groaned, easing herself back and forth. She leaned forward just enough to slide up and down his length. She grinned as he shuddered beneath her. "Thank you," she breathed.

He gripped her hips with those warm, massive hands, keeping her steady.

"Harder," she said, squeezing over his hands to tighten his grip. She braced herself on his chest and began to move in earnest.

"A ghrá,' he murmured, "A ghrá. A ghrá."

She moaned, the end turning into a whine as he started to move with her.

"I can feel you tightening."

"Oh, gods—"

"Let me wrap my fingers in this beautiful hair." He brought a hand up, curling it over the back of her neck, then used the leverage to pump up into her.

"Oh—Satyr."

"You're doing so well, a ghrá." He pumped up again, and she met him for each stroke.

She couldn't form words, could hardly think. "Satyr!"

"I want to watch you come, Elaine."

Elaine threw her head back, letting her body match his rhythm. "Don't stop. Don't stop." She rode him harder as the heat built between them. Slowly, he took more control, bracing her body with the strength in his hands and thrusting up into her. "I feel that. I feel how much you like that," her rumbled, dragging her down and pressing her into his chest. "Tell me you're mine."

"I'm yours, Satyr. I'm—ah!" Elaine cried, her body shuddering against his hold.

In an instant he'd flipped them again, and she covered her own mouth with a hand as he sought his release. Every pump was harder, stronger. He hooked a hand under her backside, angling her in a way that let him fill her impossibly more.

He pressed their foreheads together, gasping as he spoke. "I love you, Elaine."

She could not respond. She kept her hand over her mouth, trying to keep her screams of pleasure from alerting the entire inn. Even as she felt his rhythm steady out she felt her own release building again.

"I love you. I love—" He groaned, filling her, continuing to pump with every shot of warmth. The thought was enough to send her over the edge the next moment, and he sucked in a breath, pushing for a little more as her release tightened around him and she swallowed her cry.

"I love you too," she panted, as the world leaked back in. "We may end up needing thicker walls."

27

Satyr

"Be careful, it's hot." He'd brewed the tea extra long—they'd both need it. Her cheeks were still tinged with a satisfying pink, her braided hair ruffled. Soon, the morning would be filled with patrons and congratulations. Many knew Sybil well enough to be happy for the babe's arrival.

There would be time enough later to consider how they would manage moving forward. For now—tea. Food. Trellin came into the kitchen, whistling.

"Is Loddy asleep?" Satyr asked.

The boy nodded, looking crisp in a fresh tunic. "Shall I bring down the chairs?"

"Please. I'll have us all some breakfast soon. Thank you."

Trellin nodded again, and Satyr smiled at Elaine as the boy walked out.

"And not a hint of resistance," she mused, lifting a teasing eyebrow.

He grinned as he shimmied over to her, looping an arm around her waist to spin them in a circle. "Perhaps we are not as doomed as I thought," he said, pressing his forehead against hers.

"Perhaps." She let him lead as he danced them across the room.

"What do you say I send for Thorin again today? He can sing happy birthday to the little one—"

A voice echoed in the dining room. "I *said* the inn isn't open yet. What, are you daft?"

Satyr released Elaine and flew through the door, heat rising into his ears. The boy had been out of trouble for all of a single morning and he—

"Satyr." Jimbe stood in the dining room, his ostentatious, immaculate clothes out of place amongst the paper lanterns and earthenware vases that decorated the Aspen Inn. His usual, slimy smile was gone, replaced by a seriousness that turned Satyr's stomach to solid stone.

"Why is there a wagon of plants outside?"

"They're for the inn," Satyr answered. It wasn't any of his business whose they were.

The man offered him a sudden, saccharine smile. "We need to talk."

He tried not to let his worry show. "Very well." Satyr crossed his arms. "Speak."

The male's eyes flicked to Trellin. "In private. Somewhere disrespectful children won't get in the way."

Satyr faked a look around, keeping his face passive. "I see no children here."

Trellin stood up straighter even as Jimbe's countenance darkened.

"I'm selling the inn."

His first instinct was to fight. "You can't do that."

"I can."

"You can't," Satyr said firmly, shoving the panic down as far as it would go. "I own at least half of it by now."

Jimbe gave him a smug smile. "That's the thing about real estate in Arnell. The city is so popular, prices keep going up and up. The fae like to hold on to things. There's so little left for the shorter lived. A shame really."

"We had a deal."

"Handshaken, I'll remind you. And incredibly generous of me at the time. But things change, Satyr. For example, I had no idea when you took over that you'd one day turn this place into an orphanage." He spat the word. "Did you think no one would tell me? You aren't as subtle as you think. Children bring down the value of everything around them—"

"You'll get your money's worth, you prick."

Satyr whirled, and Elaine stood, as crimson as he'd ever seen her. Not even Tuskala's most deadly storms could have matched the icy wrath in her voice.

"Pardon, *miss*. But this doesn't concern you."

"Don't," she demanded, as Satyr opened his mouth to speak. "Don't give him another moment of your time." Satyr almost felt relieved as she turned her attention back to the other man. "How much for the other half of the inn?"

Realization dawned on him. "Elaine, you can't—"

"I *can't*?" she challenged. "And what would you do?"

Tears pooled in his eyes for the first time since he left home. "Elaine . . ." But he had no argument.

She stared the man down. "I said how much?"

The little cockatrice puffed out his chest. "Twenty thousand."

"That's outrageous!" Satyr sputtered, just as Elaine said, "Deal. Get it in writing and you'll have it this evening."

The fae's eyes were alight with victory. "You should let your lady do more of your negotiating, Satyr. She knows how business is done."

"Get the fuck out," Elaine answered, before Satyr could recover enough to speak. As soon as the door swung closed, he flew to her, wrapping her up, suddenly awash with tears.

"Why did you do that, Elaine? You need that coin. You didn't have to do that," he wept, grateful but ashamed that he could not save himself and the ones that relied on him.

"Satyr"—she cleared her throat—"I have never felt more at home than I have with you." She pressed her forehead to his and groaned. "Gods I should have been kinder. I didn't know if he would accept, and there's still time for him to change his mind and—"

"He will not change his mind." He pressed a wet kiss into her hair. "He would have to be mad. We should negotiate, haggle him down. We should file an official complaint. I haven't done it for this long because I was afraid of what I would lose." He lifted her chin with a finger and planted a salty kiss on her mouth. "I'm not afraid now. Let me fight for us too."

She nodded, even as he felt her body stiffen with the stress of losing the ground they'd gained. But as much as he let himself be taken advantage of, he would not allow the same for her.

"I love you," she said softly.

"I love you, Elaine. I have loved you, a ghrá." He tucked her hair back. "It means love."

She smiled. "You said you didn't know the word in common."

He grinned. "That may not have been completely true."

Her face lit with a smile, but she startled and pushed away from him as Trellin spoke. "But what if he gets mad about the complaint and goes back on the deal?"

Elaine cleared her throat. "Then . . . we will find another building."

"But what about the baby?"

Satyr's heart ached as she hesitated.

"Then the baby will learn that home can be a person," he said, grabbing her hand. "Or many."

She nodded. "And you and Loddy will have a home in us too. For as long as you need."

The boy's face softened, and he swallowed. It was too easy to forget how young he was.

Talilah appeared just as Elaine left for work. Satyr looked to Loddy, who splashed in the dishwater under the guise of helping. "Would you check if anyone out there needs any water?"

"Yes, sir!" She grabbed the pitcher of water from the counter, and Satyr winced as the weight of it made her grip unsteady.

Talilah's eyes followed the girl out the door. "She's going to spill that everywhere."

"I thought I'd see you sooner."

"There were complications."

He looked back at her, his hand busy stirring the pan in front of him. "What kind of complications?"

"Nothing I couldn't handle."

"Is everyone okay?"

She leaned against the doorway, arms crossed. "Everyone is fine, I said I handled it."

He said nothing, simply lifted an eyebrow and poured the contents of the pan onto two plates.

She rolled her eyes. "Fine. Someone was trying to collect money for "protection" on the road. We refused. They seemed eager to remind us why we might need protection. So like I said. I handled it."

Satyr sighed. It wasn't uncommon for bandits masquerading as mercenaries to offer aid to travelers, only to rob them blind and leave them for the monsters.

"I think they were from Lamel," she said.

"Well hopefully they'll go home and think twice about returning. The guard here wouldn't have been any kinder than you I'm sure."

"At least one will return. The other—" She shrugged.

Trellin came in and gave Talilah a curious look. She answered with a sharp-toothed smile.

"Would you take these?" Saytr asked him. "I'll be right out."

Trellin nodded, accepting the plates piled high with stewed meat and bread rolls before carrying them out the door.

"Child labor, one crime I never expected from you, Satyr." She grinned.

"The boy is old enough, for one. And for two. I offered to let the younger one play with her wooden figures in the pantry, but it turned out to be a terrible idea."

Naturally, Loddy had tried to 'cook,' dumping entire bottles of seasonings and flour together. He would have experimented with it, maybe pan fried some fish, but she'd tripped on her way to show him, and it all landed on the floor. She wept, and he offered the sink so she could wash her hands, which turned into a different kind of play. Clean up wasn't bad—he was plenty familiar with a broom, but he probably should have anticipated the outcome in the first place.

Talilah laughed. The sound was rare, and she smothered it as Trellin walked in again.

"The man is back. With another guy."

Satyr sighed, trying to force his shoulders down even as his worry ratcheted up. "Will you stay here and make sure this doesn't burn? Just keep stirring."

Trellin opened his mouth, likely to object.

"I will!" Loddy sang, having followed her brother in from the dining room.

Satyr and Trellin looked at each other for a moment before Trellin said, "I've got it, Loddy."

The girl moved closer. "Can I watch?"

"Yes, you can watch. But don't touch it or it'll burn your skin off."

Her eyes went wide.

Satyr went to the front, beseeching any higher being that would listen for good fortune.

Jimbe stood in the middle of the dining room, his hands tucked behind his back. "You know I really will miss this place. The cobwebs in the corners, the window coverings he never asked permission to put in. Oh, Satyr, there you are!" The fae man was all smiles. "I've brought this kind fellow from the estate management to get everything in writing. Is your—what was her name—?"

"Elaine," Satyr tried not to growl.

The estate worker nodded, extending a dark-brown hand. "I'm Herron Tideweather. Wait." He squinted through rectangle spectacles. "Did you say Elaine?" He rifled through the papers in his hand. "Oh, yes! Elaine Galliade! Wonderful woman. I'm so glad she managed to find—wait this price can't be right. There's been some kind of mistake."

The landlord's head turned on a swivel. "It's the price she agreed to."

Mr. Tideweather shook his head. "It's *well* above market value."

Jimbe beamed desperately. "The place comes decorated. Tables, chairs, beds up top. And look! Mammoth skin!"

The man looked to Satyr. "Did Elaine have a mediator look over the terms?"

Jimbe didn't give him a moment to answer. "I don't see how that's relevant to your current job, Mr. Tideweather." Despite the insult, his voice hadn't wavered from its false cheer.

Satyr crossed his arms. "No. She only had this man saying he'd sell our home from under us despite the fact I've paid for half of it by now."

The man's brows pinched deeply. "I must be confused." He turned to Jimbe. "You said you owned and were selling. That you had someone who would buy in full."

"I do own this place." The male was quickly becoming indignant. "Rent was rising! There was no way he was going to continue to be able to make the payments. Not with even more mouths to feed."

"That's all well and good, but was he renting, or *renting to own*?" Mr. Tideweather said deliberately.

Jimbe's jaw flickered as he pressed his lips together. "For all you know, he was squatting here. You've no proof otherwise."

"Is that true?" the man asked Satyr.

Satyr nodded slowly. Things were different here than they were in Tuskala. Somehow, he'd learned it quickly, but still too late.

Mr. Tideweather's face was lined with consideration. "In either case, this number is too large by half. And I can't imagine many would pay even that much. I must recommend to Elaine she look elsewhere. I told her I have plenty of places opening up further south, closer to the forest—"

"No!" said Satyr and Jimbe in tandem.

"Half is fine," Jimbe spat. "Just give me what's mine and let me wash my hands of this filth once and for all."

Satyr crossed his arms. "Elaine isn't here."

Mr. Tideweather perked up. "Oh, at this time, she'd still be at work. I'd like to get this matter cleared up without any further confusion. I think it's best we visit her there."

"Fine," Jimbe agreed through clenched teeth. "You go ahead, I'll be right out."

As Mr. Tideweather walked away, the landlord stepped closer. "You're lucky I don't report on your little operation. Just think how righteous the crown would be, finding out you've been acting under their noses all along."

"You're headed to the castle. Why don't you stop by and tell the king—Tell him that you knew," Satyr said, letting his voice lift in volume. "And the money was going straight into your pocket the entire time."

The man scoffed, his face thunderous as he looked around the room to see if there were witnesses. Trellin grinned. Mr. Tideweather made a show of studying the carved door frame.

"This isn't over," Jimbe snarled, and Satyr lifted a hand in farewell as the door slammed behind him.

28

Elaine

THE PAPERS WERE SIGNED by the end of the day. She paid less than expected by half, and Herron returned with a deed that had both their names on it. "If you ever want to sell, just let me know! I know there's a building in—"

Elaine had just shaken her head, grinning as he prattled on.

The whole walk she fiddled with the paper in her hand, her stomach conflicted. She and Satyr co-owned the inn now. Would that feel strange? Would he regret it? Would she?

"Fáilte!" he called when she opened the door, his smile wide. Thorin played in the corner.

I have to go
And ne'er return
But don't waste your heartache on me
Rain falls in rivers
On the cheeks of my love

He polished a stein. "Did Mr. Tidewater find you?"

She nodded, her throat tight as she slid the deed across the counter.

His smile faltered, sending her heart to the floor, but when he looked up his eyes were shining. "My name is on it too?" he asked, his voice soft.

"Herron made it work." Technically, she'd asked, and of course the man was happy to oblige.

Satyr hesitated. "This wasn't what you were expecting."

She reached out to clasp his forearm, her skin pale against his olive-green. "It's what I was hoping." She popped up on her toes to kiss his cheek. Satyr loved this place more than a single piece of paper could say, but in the end, it made all the difference.

His shoulders relaxed and so did she, relief prickling her eyes.

"Also"—she cleared her throat—"I have enough saved so I can rent a small home, if needed. And of course I'll continue to work at the castle, but—" He placed his warm hand over hers.

He placed a warm hand over hers. "But?"

"I think it's time we give Trellin's idea a try."

29

Satyr

Crowds lined either side of the main road, roaring as candle lit paper dragons danced above their skilled handlers. Kites gave color to the rapidly darkening sky, while tumblers and fire jugglers swept by in dazzling formation.

"Whoa, look!" Trellin pointed to a fae man covered with intricate blue paintings who balanced a sword upright on his head as he walked. Not far behind was Ayala. Her eyes pierced Satyr, and she grinned, tipping her head to Elaine and the children as she danced as if to say, "See? I was right." More jewels hung from her horns this time, jingling and catching the torchlight with every movement. Her long tail lashed like a whip in time with the song, contrasting her graceful steps.

From further down, King Galentya waved from the seat of a gilded chariot as his people greeted him with an ear-splitting shriek of enthusiasm.

"The prince and princess should be next!" Elaine told the children, her cheeks flushed.

A few more performers followed, plucking instruments or dancing with pan flutes, but Satyr shrugged at Elaine when none of the other royals made an appearance.

"Come! Let us see what we find!" Satyr all but shouted to be heard over the packed space. The parade had concluded, and the crowd quickly broke to swarm the expanded traveler's market. Stalls swept all the way down side streets, filled to bursting with goods from out of Arnell proper.

Trellin held Loddy's hand, and Satyr kept an eye on them both, pausing as they studied each booth that caught their eye. He'd given them an amount of coin, and from the way their pockets jingled he was sure Elaine gave them a bit more.

"I'll be right back!" Elaine whispered as she moved to another stall close by.

He resisted the urge to watch her walk away, already terribly affected by the joy in her luminous eyes and the feel of her warm body on his arm. When she snuck back over, she tucked a crinkling package into his pocket and a warm drink in his hand.

"Hot chocolate?" he asked, as the scent rose to caress his nose.

"And a sticky bun," she said, with a wicked grin. They'd been avoiding sugar at the inn the last few days as they adjusted to Loddy's needs—they weren't going to take any chances.

All the same, he'd happily enjoy it in the privacy of his rooms tonight.

He took a long drink, and the kids returned, gratefully taking the water she'd grabbed for them.

"What'd you get?" he asked Loddy, who proudly showed him a dragon kite.

"Tellin says we can practice it on the beach!"

Satyr smiled. He'd hardly thought to go to the beach in the light of day, but it sounded wonderful—and likely would be necessary as the summer continued to warm.

"And you?" Satyr asked, catching the boy slipping something into his trouser pocket.

"It's private," the boy said, though his eyes sparkled,

Satyr squashed the immediate rise of concerned curiosity, and nodded. "Well, it seems we are off to a good start."

They continued on with Satyr carrying their bags in one arm while Elaine leaned on the other. He whipped his head to her as she hissed in pain and skipped a few steps, taking her weight off her right foot.

"What is it?" Trellin asked, looking her up and down.

"Nothing." Thankfully her steps evened out quickly enough. "The cobblestone got me. It's these shoes, really. I'll get new ones soon."

"Satyr!" a voice called.

Gregor waved them over excitedly, his efforts doubling when he realized Elaine was there too.

"I was hoping I'd see you!" His voice was muffled as he rummaged through the storage beneath his stall.

"It's always a pleasure," Elaine answered.

The merchant leapt up, victorious. "Aha!" he declared, presenting two half-full spice bottles with a flourish. "See a need, fill a need! I asked around to all the spice merchants that made their way in. You wouldn't believe how much they wanted to charge for these! Don't worry though, I charmed them down." The man winked, and Elaine laughed as she took the paprika.

"Thank you so much, that's incredibly kind."

Satyr's massive hands dwarfed his own half-full bottle at the same time.

"I'm always kind to the kind! Though perhaps I should have left it in one spice bottle after all," the merchant offered an overly charismatic eyebrow wiggle, though he straightened as Trellin lifted an unimpressed brow. Satyr tried not to show his amusement.

Elaine did no such thing, grinning wide. "Oh, no, this is lovely because I can take some to the castle. Thank you."

The man bowed as he accepted their payments.

"We should grab something for Sybil, too," she said as they went on.

He wrapped an arm around her, happy to walk anywhere she planned to go. "And then?"

"And then we go home."

Epilogue

Three weeks later, middle of the week stock ups had become almost routine as people flocked to the inn, curious about the castle's head chef and the sudden rumors that the princess might visit. Now, it seemed Arnell had a taste for Tuskalan-mix cuisine. They were only able to do true Tuskalan meals once a week for now, because of the price of durrangin meat, but she and Satyr were happy to do it at all.

And Kelre, of course. They'd hired Kelre, the silk fae, to work the dining room, and Trellin would help until Sybil could return. The mother in question popped in often enough that Satyr grumbled about it, but it was usually on evenings like this, when Elaine could hold the babe, so she didn't mind at all.

The new addition was doing well. His name was Alvar, and he was growing fast, constantly taking in the world with wide blue eyes—with a little help of course.

Elaine smoothed down the shock of dark hair on top of his head, dancing as she hummed her favorite song, which had become his favorite lullaby. The babe's eyes had finally drifted shut, and she laid him gently in his cot below a mobile of folded paper animals that had made a mysterious appearance the day after the festival—they'd each quietly agreed not to say aloud who they suspected had snuck it in. Satyr and Elaine had gifted the dragon-speckled woolen blanket she tucked around him now.

She snuck out the room and back down the stairs to let Sybil know that he'd gone down for his second nap. The crowded dining room murmured low, the clinking of dishes and the scent of roasted meat enough to make her mouth water. Hopefully Satyr had—

"SURPRISE!" the entirety of the kitchen shouted as she walked through the door, making her all but leap out of her skin.

Trellin, Loddy, Sybil, Kelre, and even Airam clapped while Satyr turned in a rush to grab an impossibly tall, frosted cake, haphazardly decorated with edible flowers and bits of candy.

"What is this?" Elaine said, smiling wide.

"Did you think we wouldn't find out about your birthday?" Satyr asked

Tears pricked at her eyes even as her grin grew wider. "And how, exactly, did you do that?" She hadn't wanted to make a fuss about it—and they'd all been so busy anyway.

Satyr starched the back of his next as he shrugged. "Mr. Tideweather sent you a note." Elaine didn't have time to voice her confusion before he produced a portion of folded parchment.

The Estates Office would like to wish you a very happy birthday. We are grateful to have you as part of Arnell's estate family. (Present this note and get a special rate on build-it-yourself cellars!)
Warm Regards,
Herron Tideweather

Elaine's laugh came out in a woosh as Loddy flew into her legs, wrapping her in a hug. "Happy birthday, Elaine!"

"Thank you, Loddy. It's a good thing we had that healer trip because there's no way I'd be able to eat all this cake by myself! Did you get to help decorate it?"

The girl grinned and nodded before stepping aside for Airam, who held his hands out to Elaine. "Oh I'm so proud of you," he said as he squeezed her. "Running your own inn—you are living the dream."

She squeezed him back. "It's Satyr's inn, I just pop in to bug him most nights. I don't think I could give up working at the castle."

He pushed her back by her shoulders, faux serious. "Please don't, I beg you. Also, I left you something on the freezer box."

She peeked over his shoulder. It appeared there were *several* packages wrapped and sitting on the freezer box.

"How did you all have time to get gifts too?" she asked, incredulous.

Satyr swept over to press a kiss into her hair. "May I remind you I'm an expert at sourcing goods?"

Trellin handed her a plate with double portions and a soft smile. She thanked him, digging in with enthusiasm.

Kelre eyed her plate, and then Satyr. "The *chef* said he used too much marjoram, but I tried to tell him it tastes just fine." Sybil snorted.

Elaine lifted her brows, hurrying to chew before she spoke. "It's excellent, not too much at all." Durrangin meat was remarkably succulent, she'd never tasted anything quite like it, but it paired well with mashed rutabaga, and was quickly becoming one of her favorite dishes. She'd have to convince the king to try it—and the prince and Leo too, once they returned from their summer home.

"Can we cut the cake?" Loddy trilled.

Satyr called over his shoulder as he prepared what looked like every plate in the inn. "Let's let Elaine finish eating."

"No, no! Please," Elaine waved a hand for them to continue. "I'm ready, let's go ahead and cut it!"

The buzz in the dining room doubled as cake rolled out to each willing table. In the end, Satyr steered her into the crowd by her shoulders and they cheered for her in a hearty mix of well wishes. This, of course, caused her to blush bright red from the tips of her ears to her littlest toes.

Trellin and Kelre went back to filling cups and clearing dishes, while Loddy had taken a liking to Sybil, who sat at the counter, wearing a now-wide-awake Alvar wrapped snug on her chest. They'd yet to hear from Beron, but the road to the Mire Isles was long. Hopefully the man was safe.

"Elaine!" Sybil called, drawing her from the fray. "I wanted to give you this."

Elaine sat next to her, contemplating the tiny, wrapped box. "You really didn't have to get me anything."

Sybil smiled, the expression somehow gentler than before. "Just open it."

The top slipped off easily, and Loddy leaned over to get an excited peek. The necklace was simple. A silver circle secured to a long, thin chain.

"What's it say?" Loddy asked.

But Elaine was already shaking her head. She couldn't read it aloud or she'd cry in front of the entire room. "Help me put it on?" she asked, turning it and looping it around her neck. Sybil obliged and embraced her.

"Thank you," Elaine murmured, squeezing tight, unable to put more than that into words.

"Are we doing gifts?" Satyr asked, sweeping up to put a large hand on her shoulder. "I'll be right back."

He slipped in and out of the kitchen with a grin and approached her with one hand held behind his back. "Left or right?"

She scoffed lightheartedly, but he lifted an eyebrow, unrelenting.

"Fine. That one," she said, pointing to his left.

He swept that arm out, revealing an empty hand that he flourished before reaching for her braid, which he tugged, pulling her in for a quick kiss. "Guess again."

Her cheeks ached from so much smiling. When was the last time her cheeks had ached from smiling? "Alright, then the other."

He brandished a wooden spatula, completely ordinary except for the heart cut out of the handle. His voice was soft. "To match the one from your sister."

She nodded. "It's beautiful, Satyr."

"I had it engraved," he said, gesturing for her to turn it over.

She snorted. "Cooking is my love language?"

"Your words, not mine." He nuzzled his nose to hers.

"Thank you," she said, nuzzling right back. "Did Airam go already?"

"Mmhmm. Said he needed to get back to his husband." She opened her mouth to speak, but he pushed on—"and yes I sent him with extra cake."

She whacked him with the spatula.

"I'm next then."

Elaine startled into a laugh as Trellin all but manifested right next to her. The boy moved quieter than anyone she knew. "Trellin! You should have saved your coin! You never have to buy me anything."

He pressed the box into her hands. "It's part of birthdays. Besides—you needed them."

She needed them? She felt the confusion on her face but couldn't imagine what in the world she could need at this moment. She had everything she'd ever wanted over the course of the day. Most of it still sat in this room.

"Well, go on." Sybil pat the babe's back as she rocked.

Elaine lifted the top and pushed the brown wrapping paper out of the way.

Shoes. In the box, was a pair of her shoes. Almost the exact same color and cut, but the firm leather shined, and the stitching was new.

The boy beamed, his pride like a beacon. "Stole a pair from your house this morning to make sure I got the right size—"

The words cut off as she wrapped him in a fierce hug. Satyr's laugh boomed through the inn as he scooped his massive green arms around them all. Trapped in the middle, Elaine cried, the sweet, forever ache in her chest balanced by the weight of a silver charm.

Still good.

Home

The water she sees me
  The waves bid me come
  Come and then be free
  Her beckoning hum
  Were I to go
  I'd never return
  The water, its song
  Bid me stay
  Stay and don't suffer
  For the absence of land
  Nought but heartache lay that way
  I knew a girl
  Both witty and fair
  Lips pink as rosebuds and
  Black as night hair
  She said to go
  And ne'er return
  The heartache, its song
  Bid me stay
  But stay and I'll suffer
  For the absence of her

When she's but an arm's length away

Find me in rainfall
Find me in tears
Find me in this song
Whenever you hear
I have to go
And ne'er return
But don't waste your heartache on me
Rain falls in rivers
On the cheeks of my love
But always returns to the sea

Acknowledgements

As always, this book wouldn't exist without the Coven. Jemma Croft, Sarah C. Davies, Lex Easton, Stephanie Beverly, Ana Miki, and Ellen, literally you guys changed my life for the better. I'm so grateful to be surrounded by talented, loving authors that have taught me the magic of memes, donuts, hoses, and beta readers.

Thank you, Sarah C. Davies and Lex Easton, for being my always-thorough beta readers and helping this book grow into what it was meant to be.

Thank you to Pebbles, for being the best book wife. And thank you to every single person in the writing community—all my writing sprint friends (you know who you are!) who show up with me in the mornings to get these books on the page. I only know I can do this because you encourage and teach me every day. Thank you to Atlas Creed for Indie Author Connect, the pool of resources (and your time and labor!) are invaluable.

Thank you to the cast and crew of The Long Rest, especially the writing group I have the honor of working beside. Cody,

Patrick, Kyler, and Z, you all have incredible minds and incredible talent. I never thought I would look forward to meetings so much.

Thank you to my husband, Landon, for being my biggest fan and reading the entirety of this book during a single shift while you were at work. Oh, and for witnessing all the tears and my glee at the single pun in this book.

For all eternity I will thank our two babes R and E, for remaining patient and encouraging while I lose my mind diving into this world of paper and ink.

And if you're still reading, thank you. I wrote this for you. I hope you like it.

Megan G. Mossgrove is the author of The Sundered Stone series. She's a line editor, loves writing poetry, and writes as part of the team for The Long Rest, a fantasy audio drama. When not absorbed with writing, she grows flowers and plays videogames with her husband and their two feral children.

Scan for Socials, Website, and More!